BRUTAL SINNER

A REAPER ROMANCE

STELLA ANDREWS

BRUTAL SINNER

Sinners don't belong in a town called Heaven
A place governed by the church which controls through fear.

Then the Devil rolled into town dressed in leather and a bad attitude.

We bumped heads one day outside the store and as my eyes met his, he trapped
my soul.

He was dangerously forbidden, with glittering eyes that burned right through me and scorched my heart.

I was immediately under his spell because nobody had ever looked at me like that.

It was temptation of the most devastating kind.

The sparks flew between us, but I was the only one burning.

I had committed the ultimate sin and would be punished for my crimes before
the entire town.

So, I ran.

Away from him, away from Heaven, my family, and my punishment.

But I couldn't run from the consequences.

Seven months later, they found me and brought me back with my baby.

My only chance at salvation was to marry Reverend Peters. The crazy,

sadistic brute who promised to beat the devil from my soul.

When you burn your bridge, you better hope you're on the right side because

one week before my wedding Hell rides into Heaven and we are all about

to burn.

For fans of second-chance romance with a secret baby, who love dangerously sexy men about to tear Heaven apart to protect the woman they love.

PROLOGUE

*S*omething is very wrong. My entire body burns. I expected it to be painful, but that was excruciating. However, none of it mattered when I held my daughter in my arms for the first time. The bond of motherhood cemented my heart in place, and it was insta love of the sweetest kind. The way she stared at me as if she knew who I was drove so much emotion inside me I thought I would burst. At that moment, when I met my daughter for the very first time, I missed Jonny so much it physically hurt.

I denied him that moment. He will never forgive me and as I stared into my daughter's eyes, I whispered her name. *Hope*.

It was never going to be anything else because she is my miracle from God. She has given me everything to live for and I will fight to the death to keep her.

I remember those emotions now as I lie with my eyes tightly shut, hoping like crazy I'm just having a nightmare.

They're here.

Before I even open my eyes, I know that. The deep voice

of the man who makes my skin crawl sounds too close to be a hallucination.

A million needles prickle against my skin as I wake up to the realization they found us.

If I don't open my eyes, they won't be there. They'll disappear in a cloud of smoke and I'll be safe again.

"Faith!"

The sharp command from the man who calls himself my father causes me to shiver in fear and the prayer for the damned is ringing in my ears as Reverend Peters prays for my soul.

"Dear Lord. Thank you for your forgiveness. Thank you for not abandoning us to our mistakes, but for reaching out instead to bring us home."

Home.

House of monstrous evil.

That's what those letters stand for, and they always have.

The word fills me with terror and only the sudden realization I don't hear my baby causes my eyes to snap open as I sit up with a start.

"Hope."

I stare around me wildly and note the empty crib by my bed and I shout, "Where is my fucking baby!"

My parents visibly wince and hold their hands together in prayer and the reverend carries on chanting some kind of psalm for the damned.

"Where have you taken her?"

I make to leave and am shocked when my father forces me back and pins me to the bed with an aggressive sneer.

"On her way to Heaven."

"What are you talking about?" I scream and wonder where the fuck the medical staff is and then Reverend Peters yells. "ENOUGH!"

He turns to me and says icily, "Repent sinner, you are

damned along with your bastard child. The only way to salvation is to repent of your sins and face your punishment."

"My punishment?" I stare at my mom through terrified eyes, but my only concern is where Hope is.

"Faith." Her voice rains down on me like acid as she stares at me with sad disappointment.

"Don't be a fool. You are in no position to care for a child. Come home with us and we will help you."

"Help me?" I stare at her in shock, and she nods. "The reverend has agreed that you may return and care for your child under our watchful eye. You have no choice."

"Where is she?" I say it calmly, as if I'm talking to people with no rational thought and I really don't believe they have any.

My father says tightly, "She is with Goody. Come home, Faith, and don't make a scene. You've caused enough trouble already."

As I buckle under the weight of their hostile expressions, my world tips on its axis. The walls close in on me and I struggle to breathe because my fight is far from over. They found me and taken the one thing I will never abandon, and so I nod meekly, knowing there is no other choice.

However, I've tasted freedom once and will again. I'll bide my time and work out a plan because one thing is definite, my trip home will be a temporary one.

CHAPTER 1

FAITH

NINE MONTHS LATER

A shiver passes through me and it's not because of the temperature. It could be a blazing hot day and I would still feel cold.

I wish I hadn't come. Not that I was given the choice, but now I'm here, I wish I had run and never looked back.

"Stand up straight, Faith."

My father nudges me and I stand to attention as always.

The scene before me is morbid, sad, and inevitable and as tragedies go, this one doesn't surprise me.

"Ashes to ashes…"

The dull rumble from the priests' repertoire signifies the poor soul being laid to rest and as we all say "amen" I watch the chief mourner step forward, causing a murmur of reverence to pass through the crowd.

He holds a single white rose in his hand, and he makes a big show of tossing it into the open grave as if he cared for the person inside.

There are no tears at this funeral. There is nobody present who would dare show a hint of emotion.

He steps back and then turns, a solitary figure who surrounds himself with power. He demands respect and reverence and I'm still wondering if the crowd are merely good actors because, from the expressions on their faces, they idolize him.

I stand straight and tall, my hands clasped before me as if in a silent prayer for the soul of the persecuted woman who is better off where she is.

Agatha Peters. Wife of Reverend Peters, the man who presides over the souls of the residents of Heaven. A man who believes he has that right and that God chose him personally. A man who can do no wrong, according to his congregation and any outsiders who stroll into town are soon offered nothing but the route out of here.

Heaven is a place on earth that is Hell disguised within an angel's wings. There is nothing good about living in Heaven and I'm the fool who thought she could escape.

"Stand up straight, Faith. He's coming."

I watch the reverend move away from the open grave and note the expression on his face is somber with no emotion. Surely, he should be devastated. His wife is dead but word in the shadows is she went there voluntarily. Once again, I shiver as the man steps even closer and as he draws near, I cast my eyes to the ground, fearful of looking the monster in the eye. If I don't see him, he's not there. I wish that was true because he is so close now, I almost can't breathe. There is a toxicity about Reverend Peters that surrounds him and my heart races as he reaches us and, more than anything, I pray he passes us by so I can breathe again.

He doesn't.

No words are spoken, but he stops and a black gloved

finger, tips my face to stare into eyes that flash with something I'm going to pretend I haven't seen.

"Name."

He barks and my mom says in a reverent whisper, "Faith, sir."

"Does it speak?"

I feel the anger burning inside and note the small twist to his lips and the challenge flashing in his eyes as mom says quickly, "Faith. Say something."

The challenge hangs in the air along with bated breath as they wait for me to speak, and my voice comes out with a strong overload of sarcasm as I say through gritted teeth. "I am sorry for your loss, sir."

His grip tightens on my chin and as I make to pull away, he leans forward and his breath dances way too close for comfort. "My loss is your gain."

My mother gasps as he flicks his malevolent gaze at my father and says dismissively, "I have a vacancy for a wife. Bring her to my home at seven tonight. We will talk then."

He drops my chin and as I make to speak, he lays the flat of his gloved hand across my mouth and hisses, "Do not speak, girl and listen. You are a sinner and require work to cleanse your soul. I am the only one who can help you."

He leans forward and whispers in my ear. "Before you contemplate any other answer than thank you, I have something of yours you may want back."

An icy sensation crawls through my entire body as his meaning hits home. The demons scream and cackle in glee as they fly around my soul, dragging it into their evil hands as they prepare to deliver me to evil.

The rage inside me burns fiercer than the pit of hell as I understand his meaning and as he drops my face, he says to my father. "Don't be late."

He moves past and I step back as if his touch burned,

longing to tear off my clothes and jump into the shower to rid myself of his touch. I make to flee, to run, to escape, but his parting shot was the door to my cage crashing shut.

Mom reaches for my hand and says in a low whisper, "It's for the best, Faith."

"You knew?"

My voice is tearful, destroyed even, and she nods, the sadness in her eyes the only indication she has any emotion left inside her.

My father growls, "You are being given a second chance, Faith. Don't ruin this one."

"Daddy, please." I say in a voice that sounds weak and pathetic and he says icily, "You heard him. Seven o'clock Faith. Go home and pack."

"Pack?"

It's as if a storm came out of nowhere and is carrying me off and as the line of mourners passes, I wish I could run the other way. I don't miss their curious glances and the distaste on their faces as they pass. I half expect them to spit on me. I wouldn't put it past them because of what I did.

My parents act as the harshest prison guards as they escort me from the grave and we follow the line of mourners heading to the church to pray for Agatha's soul. There will be no wake. No party to celebrate her life. Just more prayers and lamenting for the sinners we are.

The church stands on the edge of the cemetery and as we head inside the white wooden building, I wish I could run. I already know I can't because of what I did. My secret that in Heaven's eyes is my cross to bear and as we step into the cold church, it's as if I am dragging my sin behind me like a ball and chain.

Rather than take our usual seats, we head toward the front. The curious stares of the congregation watching us as we make our silent journey. Our usual seats have been filled already and the only person I register is my best friend Purity, and her look of horror matches my own.

We reach the front of the church and I regard the empty pew in the direct view of a tyrant, who is standing in his pulpit watching our progression with a hard, contemplative expression.

As we shuffle into the row, he says loudly, "It is done. Today we lament the passing of my wife Agatha Peters. A woman who strove to be the perfect wife and was assured of her ascendency to Heaven. Now my work continues, and I am needed to cleanse a wicked soul. To bring light into darkness and right the wrongs of the past."

He stares at the congregation and says in a voice that seals my death sentence.

"After ten days of mourning, I will marry again. My chosen is Faith Monroe, who fell into wickedness. I will take the burden on and drive her demons away in honor of Agatha's memory. She will be my biggest success and will benefit from my understanding. It is settled. Praise be to the lord."

I don't even register the opening bars of the closing hymn because my mind is racing faster than a rocket to the moon. Marry him!

Like hell I will, and I have ten days to figure a way out of this nightmare or else I may as well go and lie on top of his poor departed wife and cut out the middle man. If I have done the math right, Reverend Peters has just buried wife number four and I'm almost certain they will be already preparing the ground beside her for the next in line.

Me.

CHAPTER 2

JONNY

*T*he scent of leather and diesel reminds me of home, and I take a deep breath and wish I was there.

Like a fool, I made a decision that is probably a bad one and am taking a few days to head to my former home.

I grew up in Heaven. A small town lost among rugged terrain with the neighboring town a day's drive away.

I couldn't wait to get out and was never intending on going back except for unfinished business that, as hard as I try, just won't remain the past.

"She's ready."

The gruff tones of the mechanic make me look up and he stands back with an expression of pride as he reveals his latest masterpiece.

I stand, the pull of the machine too great as I cast my eyes over the gleaning chrome of the Harley who is soon to become my girl.

I step forward and run my hand over the leather and love the cold steel against my palm. Desire bubbles inside me for what this girl can do, and I long to feel her between my legs as I ride her hard.

There is nothing I don't adore about this machine and can't wait to hear her purr under me.

"She's good to go."

The mechanic growls, a mixture of amusement and jealousy on his face as he watches my reaction.

I toss him my credit card and take a moment alone with my latest love while he transfers the funds.

Freedom. This is what she gives me and what I crave, like a cold beer on a sun-drenched day.

He returns and tosses me the keys along with the card and says with pride. "Unlike a woman, she won't give you no trouble."

His words stir the beast inside me because only one woman has ever given me trouble, which is the reason I'm heading back home in the first place.

"That's good to know."

I offer him a lopsided grin as I swing my leather clad leg over the bike, relishing the steel between my legs and as I zip up my battered leather jacket, I reach for the helmet.

"Where are you heading?" He says, making conversation and I grin.

"Heaven."

He raises his eyes.

"They don't hand out warm welcomes in Heaven. Not to a man like you, anyway."

He chuckles softly, and I shrug.

"I'm not there on vacation. It's business."

"In Heaven?" He laughs out loud.

"Then you would be better pulling on a suit and taking a cab. They won't want to do business with the likes of you."

His words could easily offend, but I take it as a compliment. The last thing I want is to be anything like the people who live there. In fact, I have made it my mission to be everything they draw the shutters closed on as they pray for my soul, because the second I step into town, I will have a target on my back.

They hate me.

They disowned me a couple of years back and I vowed never to return and there is only one reason why I broke that vow, and it goes by the name of Faith.

"So, what business are in you in?" The guy says with interest, and I grin, "War."

He raises his eyes. "I take it back. You are heading in the perfect direction for that."

I turn the ignition and the machine roars into life, and I swear I could come so hard at that sound. It's been a while and I almost groan out loud as the beast throbs between my thighs, impatient to hit the open road.

He steps back and grins. "Have fun."

"I intend to." Laughing to myself, I guide the beast toward the open road and open the throttle.

I'm back.

Heaven won't know what's hit it when the Brutal Sinner rides into town and if anyone stands in my way of answers, they will wish they were anywhere else.

I stop three times on my way to Heaven. Once to pick up supplies, once to refuel and once to grab some refreshment.

As the sign comes into view, it makes me smile.

WELCOME TO HEAVEN

Stopping, I reach inside my leather jacket and my fingers close around the object I'm searching for and as I step off the bike, I head toward the sign and grin.

With one quick movement of my hand, I draw a black line through Heaven with permanent marker and write Hell in its place.

Yes, this place has always been hell to me and should be prosecuted for misleading the public. It has never been Heaven; it's always been Hell and this time the devil is riding into town on a horse of steel to shatter some souls.

I take a quick pic of my handiwork and send it to the bastard who persuaded me to take this trip, and I grin when the text is returned with the words.

Then you're in the right place, soldier.

I take a moment to appreciate the man who took me in. Ryder King. President of The Twisted Reaper MC and the man I would die to protect. A bad-assed ex-military assassin who left and formed the club we all live and die by.

We work for the government under the disguise of leather and devil intent and take out those who threaten our constitution. When the law fails, we step in, and I relish tossing the bad guys on the devil's inferno in the afterlife.

When I left the military, I was sent straight there by my commanding officer. He told me they would have a home for me, and he was right. I live at the Rubicon and work for my brothers and there is nowhere else I would rather be. They gave me a freedom I've never had, and it's a powerful drug for a man who has never experienced that. However, there is one thing from my past that I just can't shake and it's the reason why the woman I loved ran from me. She disappeared and no matter how hard I searched, she remained hidden and only when her best friend told me she had run from me did I stop looking.

It hurt. It destroyed, and it set me on my current path and I headed back to the military, where I vented my anger for the good of the country. I was out of control, which led to my commanding officer recommending a different kind of army and I never regretted the transition.

Now it's time to head home for a visit and I wonder what they will think of the man I became.

If I know my parents, they will pray for my soul and with a slight chuckle, I step back on my bike and prepare myself for a homecoming that none of us will be celebrating.

CHAPTER 3

FAITH

*A*s soon as we are home, I turn on my parents angrily. "I won't do it."

The fear in my mother's eyes tells me I've pushed them too far and my father roars, "You will do what we tell you, girl!"

"Cyrus, no."

Mom says quickly as he raises his hand to me and as he lowers it, he says icily, "You need a strong hand, girl, and I regret treating you so good. You threw it all back in our face when you—"

"Stop. Please." Mom says with a sob, and I wonder why she's bothering. Men don't listen to the women in Heaven because it's always been all about them.

He says with a warning in his voice, "Now go and pack. You've been given a second chance to redeem yourself in the eyes of the lord and Reverend Peters is a saint for taking you on."

"A saint?" I make to argue, but the warning in my mom's eyes freezes the words in an instant.

I won't win this argument. Not with them. I never will

because a child is owned by their parents in Heaven. They are made to do what they want and if you go against the code we live by you are an outcast. I should know, I'm one of them and my thoughts turn to the reason I'm in this mess in the first place.

"Where is she?"

My father steps in front of my mother and says with a sigh.

"It's for your own good, Faith. Both of you."

"Where is she?" I hiss and he yells, "Where you are going and be thankful he is taking you both on. You are lucky he is so generous."

"Where is she!" I scream and mom says quickly, "With Reverend Peters."

"How?"

"When we were at Church. It was arranged."

I step back as if they slapped me and my walls crumble under the biggest betrayal.

"You planned this. How long?"

I step toward them, and my father pushes me back so hard I stumble.

"Yes!" He roars. "We planned it. This is the best of a bad situation. Who else would take you on with a bastard child?"

This time I run at him and am rewarded with a punch to my stomach. I drop to my knees as my mom cries and my father yells, "You are a whore! The devil took your soul and corrupted you. No man wants to marry a whore and you are lucky the Reverend is a holy man and has vowed to punish the devil inside you."

It hurts so much, but I won't cry. Not in front of them because any tears I had dried up years ago.

Mom says gently, "Please, Faith. This is the best situation for all of us."

I stare up at her and whisper, "All of us?"

"Yes."

She drops to her knees before me and sobs, "You let this family down. You had sex with a man and bore a child out of wedlock. We are pariahs in this town because of you, and this will help us get our reputation back."

She grasps my hands. "You will be the wife of the most influential man in Heaven. His *wife*, Faith. You will be powerful by association, and so shall we. Reverend Peters has done this family a great honor and only a fool would refuse. You have no choice—there is *no* other choice, so do as your father says and pack your bags. Do it for Hope if you won't do it for you. Please, I'm begging you."

The person staring at me with obvious distress is a stranger to me. I suppose she always has been because she gave up being a mother years ago. When I think of my own daughter currently in the hands of a monster, I realize there is only one choice. She is the most important thing in my life, and I will fight for her.

They may believe this war is over, but I'm a fighter and this is not sitting well with me. I have a child and responsibilities and if they think I'm going to play by their rules, then they don't know me at all. I never have and when I found a man of the same mind, we destroyed one another.

We clashed like two bolts of lightning and the explosion rocked this small town. He was always bad news, always a renegade, and that was the main attraction. Every girl loves a bad boy and Jonny Santos was the devil to whom I readily gifted my soul.

I have no choice and as I pack, I gulp back the tears, determined to keep a cool head rather than react.

As I fill the cases, I swallow back the tears as I fold the cute little garments that Hope looks so sweet in. A gentle tap on the door almost passes me by because my own thoughts

17

are so loud I can hear nothing else and then as the door opens, our house maid Goody heads in and says with great sadness, "I'm so sorry Miss."

"I hate you."

I stand and stare at the poor maid as she cowers under my icy glare.

"I had no choice." She offers by way of an explanation, and I hiss, "You gave them my child. How could you?"

The tears run down her face as she whispers, "I had to. You understand that Miss. It's how things work around here."

I know I'm being a bitch. Blaming the hired help for something she has no control over and with a sigh, I drop down on the bed and say sorrowfully, "What am I going to do, Goody?"

"Beats me." She sighs heavily and sits beside me and takes my hand in a show of compassion.

"It may not be so bad, ma'am."

"Do you really believe that?"

I half laugh and she shakes her head mournfully. "No, ma'am. I guess you're right."

"He's so old, Goody." I shiver as I contemplate the man who will call himself my husband.

"He is."

Her voice trembles and I sigh heavily. "So ugly too."

"He is, Miss."

"You don't suppose I'll have to…"

I can't even say the words and Goody squeezes my hand a little tighter. "I'm so sorry, Miss."

"I'm screwed, aren't I, Goody?"

"Yes, Miss." She doesn't even try to pretend, which makes me smile. I always could rely on Goody to say it how it is.

"I'll miss you, Goody." I lean against her, and she says softly, "Me too, Miss. Faith."

I cast my eyes around the room and note the small piles

of clothes. There isn't much because possessions are considered the bounty of the devil. We exist on the bare minimum and so I'm sure that all my worldly goods would fit into one small case. Hope's things will probably take another one.

Goody says apologetically. "I was sent to help you pack."

"That's ok, thanks."

I watch as she begins packing my things with care and I wander across to the window and stare outside on a back yard that is practical rather than a pleasure to look at.

I catch sight of a glint in the distance and say quickly, "I'm just going to grab some fresh air. I won't be long."

"Are you sure they will allow that, Miss?"

Goody sounds worried and I sigh. "If I could run anywhere I would, but there is nowhere to run in Heaven. I tried that once and look where it got me."

She nods. "Of course, Miss."

Rather than face my parents again, I open the window and drop the short distance to the ground. As I take off across the yard, I head to the stream that runs at the bottom of the field.

As I reach it, I'm happy to see I wasn't wrong, and my friend Purity races toward me with a horrified expression.

"This is a disaster."

"You're telling me."

She pulls me into her arms and holds on tight.

"What are we going to do?"

"I'm open to all suggestions." I say with a groan and pull her down on the edge of the bank and flick a stone into the river.

"I could drown myself, but what about Hope?"

"Is it true?"

"What?"

"That they took her when we were at church."

"Who told you that?"

I'm interested more than anything and she shakes her head. "Everyone knew, it seems. Everyone but me and you and I expect they never told me because they guessed I'd warn you."

"I hate them all."

I huff and draw my knees to my chest.

"Tell me what to do, Purity?"

She says in a sad voice. "They've made it so you don't have time. You can't escape because everyone knows where you're heading and would stop you leaving."

"We could try, though." I say thoughtfully.

"I mean, I have ten days. Maybe just go along with it while we plan our escape."

"We?" Purity sounds nervous, and I nod with a growing determination.

"Yes us, Purity. It's only a matter of time before you're manipulated in the same way. I'm guessing they've already chosen your husband and you will live an empty life with a man you don't love."

"I know." She sounds worried, and she has every right to be because there are slim pickings in Heaven on the husband front as most of the men here are brainwashed their entire lives and believe a woman's place is under them and then waiting on them.

We both turn at the same time and share the same expression, which makes us smile and I reach for her hand and whisper, "I'll need your help. Leave it with me and I'll find a way and this time there will be no mistakes."

CHAPTER 4

JONNY

The house is empty, which suits me just fine. I chose this time because, as always, like clockwork, my parents will be at church praying for my soul with a righteous pomposity that they've worn like a cloak their entire life.

As I wander around the familiar rooms, it makes my blood run cold as past demons circle me with memories of a bitter past.

They tried so hard to wear me down. To indoctrinate me in the ways of this tainted town, but somewhere deep inside I wanted more. I always knew there was more, and I suppose the anger built to a point where it destroyed me.

This isn't my first homecoming. When I returned from the military, I bumped into Faith, literally, and I'm guessing her parents wished I never had. We were an explosion that rocked this town, and I would have killed for her.

To this day I still don't know why she ran from me, and it hurt—so damned hard. My pride took a battering along with my heart and after a colossal row with my folks, I was sent packing with mom's words ringing loud in my ears. She told me there was no place in Heaven for a man who murders innocent people. She called me a sinner. A brutal sinner who deserved to burn in hell for his crimes. Then my father disowned me and told me I was no child of theirs and to never come back.

Well, shit happens, I guess, and a wry smile ghosts my lips as I prepare for their reaction to the prodigal son showing his face once again.

I fix myself a coffee and carry it from room to room, familiarizing myself with a house that was never a home. The bare minimum with no fancy edges. A lot like every home in Heaven because possessions are the Devil's work.

I kick open the door to my room and stare with interest at the single bed and simple cotton curtains billowing at the open window overlooking the corn fields. No skyscrapers here, no coffee shops or bars. Just open land to cleanse a person's soul.

It's my own personal hell.

The bare floorboards creak under the weight of my boot and the air is still as it waits for rare drama to unfold.

The painted walls are stark, with no pictures or mirrors to please the eye, definitely no mirrors because staring at your reflection is considered vanity, which has no place here.

To be honest, I'm wondering why I'm here at all. I don't belong here; I never did, but it's a starting point, I guess.

I finish up my coffee and head to the stark kitchen and rinse my mug under the trickle of water before setting it down to drain. Sighing inside, I stare out at the yard and remember many hours playing there as a child. Alone.

I never really thought about it, but now I'm back, it saddens me. There is a strict one child policy in Heaven. Any more is considered careless. As a result, I played alone for most of my life, making my own entertainment as my mind went slowly mad. Even at school, we sat at single desks and friendships were frowned upon because they believed it distracted our minds from education. It angers me when I think of my life now. The friends I have that are more like brothers and the richness they bring to my life.

My jacket rests like a comforting arm around my shoulder. A gentle pack on the back and a silent friend by my side. The club's emblem is emblazoned across the back, and it makes me smile. The Grim Reaper sits on my back and is inked on my arm.

Twisted Reaper MC is written on my back, both on the jacket and again on my shoulders. I am branded and belong to a very exclusive club that stands for a whole lot of honor and sacrifice. I'm used to that; I can live with dedicating my life to my brothers, but it appears I can't live without one more chance with Faith.

I hear the car making its way to the front porch and wonder with interest what their reaction will be. They will already know the devil is in town from my girl out the front, gleaming in the sunlight as she makes a powerful statement outside.

I can imagine their hearts dropping and the nerves jangling. Anger for sure and a desire to get rid of their visitor before anyone else discovers I'm here.

I take a seat at the simple wooden table facing the door and wait with interest to watch them walking through it.

Their footsteps are slow and heavy, even now they move around like demons with chains on their soul. Almost robotic with no mind of their own and I wonder if I would be the same if I hadn't discovered a mind of my own.

The door opens and I stare into the narrowed eyes of my father, who is wearing his distaste for everyone to see. I peer past him and note the pinched face of my mother as she glances my way with a worried frown.

"Leave."

A simple word that tells me exactly where I stand, and I shrug.

"It's good to see you too, sir, ma'am."

I address them formally because I've never called them anything else. Certainly not ma or pa because they never deserved that title. Respect for your elders includes your parents and the kids in Heaven speak to everyone as if they are strangers. I suppose they are really, and family is stranger than most and so the devil in me dances around the room with glee as I lean back and regard them through narrowed eyes.

My father sighs and says over his shoulder, "Ida, fix me some refreshment."

She scurries past him and as her hand reaches for the kettle, I note the shake of her hand as she fills it with water.

My father sits opposite me and says sternly, "State your business."

"I'm on vacation, sir, and thought I'd check on you."

"And your real business."

His response makes me laugh softly because I never could get anything past this man.

"Faith."

A loud noise distracts our attention as mom drops the kettle in the sink and my father says roughly, "Shape up, Ida, don't be so clumsy."

"Don't speak to her like that." I growl and I'm not sure who is more shocked, my father or my mother who catches my eye and I'm surprised to witness the tears in her eyes before she looks away and refills the kettle.

"You dare to challenge me in my own home?"

My father's voice is deep and emotionless, and I sigh heavily, resisting the urge to place my booted feet on their table in an act of defiance that even I can't bring myself to perform.

"She's a woman, sir. They deserve our respect."

"Since when?"

My father shakes his head. "They deserve nothing. They earn respect by cleaning the home and caring for the men. That is how it works in Heaven, or have you forgotten that already?"

He doesn't wait for my answer and says shortly, "Faith is not your concern. She is not here, so leave."

I stare at him with a cold calculating look and the air is so icy I'm glad I have my trusted leather on my back.

"Interesting." I lean forward and stare at him with an expression of no shit.

"She is no concern of mine, you say."

"You heard me, boy."

The fact I tower over him, and my muscles make me double his size, renders his statement almost laughable.

"Then why not just tell me she isn't here?"

For the first time in my entire life, my father shows nerves. The fact I have been trained so well these past few years tells me that. I have learned to read facial expressions and realize when someone is lying to me, and he definitely is. I stare at him hard, and he withers under its ferocity as a bead of sweat forms on his brow and he licks his lips with a nervous reaction.

The moment is gone when mom slams a plate on the table with three dry biscuits and says nervously, "Coffee is ready."

He nods and breaks eye contact and as mom sits down nervously beside him, I don't miss the pain in her eyes as she tries hard not to look at me.

It hurts me so deep because mom has always appeared a broken piece of china with jagged edges. Once a thing of great beauty that has been uncared for. Her beautiful pattern faded over the years and the cracks glued together with yellowing adhesive. I wonder what God would think if he walked the streets of Heaven. Not a lot, I'm guessing, and it makes me madder than I thought it would.

An uneasy silence sits between us while we try to figure one another out and as I sip the bitter coffee, I am only glad for its caffeine shot.

I'm surprised when my father breaks the silence and says with a sneer, "It appears you fell even harder. Congratulations on reaching rock bottom."

I'm guessing he is referencing my appearance and I smile, proud of who I became.

"You mean my club, I suppose."

"Is that what you call it?" He shakes his head in distaste.

"A biker. Why am I not surprised?"

Mom shares his disdainful look and I know she will never understand the life I lead. Loud, rough men and soft, pretty whores. A den of iniquity to some. I call it home.

"Yes." I raise a small smile. "I'm a biker, sir, and proud of it."

"You can't stay here." Is his bleak response and I shrug.

"I doubt I'd fit the bed, anyway."

I laugh softly and stand, the air too toxic to be of any benefit to me.

"It's good to see you." I lie as I move to the door, loving the horror on my parent's faces as the full regalia of my jacket reveals itself.

Mom gasps as dad hisses, "You wear the devil on your back in plain sight."

I grin and turn, fixing my expression to bastard and hiss, "According to you, I always did, so why pretend anymore?"

"So, you're leaving?" The hope in mom's voice drives that rusty knife that's always lived in my heart a little deeper and I push the pain away and shake my head. "Why would I leave when I've only just got here?"

"Where are you going?" I don't miss the fear in her voice as I start walking, not even bothering to answer her.

The scrape of a chair alerts me and as my father comes up behind me, I turn so we are standing eye to eye and he hisses, "I am warning you, leave. There is nothing for you here."

"Then I'll be the judge of that." I hiss back before turning away and saying as an aside. "Thanks for the hospitality. As always, it's been a blast."

I walk away from my parents with no emotion at all. Sometimes I wonder where I'm really from because surely, it's not from them. I have nothing in common with them at all which I'm glad about. I always have felt like the stranger within and if I could be bothered, I may investigate that a little more, but I can't. The only thing that bothers me now is answers and there is only one person who can give me them and so, with a heart full of rage and a mind filled with dark intent, I leave my childhood home behind and sit astride the new woman in my life, who will undoubtedly never let me down.

CHAPTER 5

FAITH

I don't have long. When I left Purity, I headed home with a heavy heart. Seven pm tonight and everything will change. I will be a man's possession. A wife in training and it's almost comical dwelling on modern day in Heaven when we could well be in the past.

My thoughts turn to the one time I stepped out of my comfort zone and left. The bright lights of the city beckoned, but I didn't get far. Afraid, lost, and angry, I went to the nearest town that was a metropolis compared to our small town. I was a sinner. I had done the unthinkable and tossed my virginity to the devil himself. I wish I could say I regret it, but I'd be lying. I would do it again in a heartbeat and I will *never* regret bringing my daughter into the world.

It's why I must be strong now. For her. For us and I owe it to her to come up with a plan allowing us to leave forever.

Goody is finishing up, and she regards me with a desolate expression.

"I will be ok, Goody." I smile to reassure her as well as myself and she shakes her head and for once speaks out of turn.

"It's not right, ma'am."

"Has it ever been right?"

I raise my brow and she nods. "I suppose."

"What about you, Goody? Have you ever wanted to marry?"

I'm interested because Goody isn't that much older than me.

"I would like that very much." Her eyes sparkle, which causes me to peer a little deeper because, well, I'll be. Our maid is more devious than I thought.

"Who is he?" I lower my voice and her startled expression makes me draw closer and whisper, "It will be our secret."

Her face turns crimson as she giggles and whispers, "Edward, ma'am."

"The gardener?"

She nods. A secretive smile on her face.

"He told me he was going to ask my father to arrange a marriage between us."

Once again, our dictatorial ways come back and bite me because the women of Heaven never get to choose. It's always the men and yet, in Goody's case, she appears more than happy about that.

"When?" I ask with a happy smile, and she grins.

"One week from today."

"Why wait?" I'm confused, and she says sadly.

"We cannot ask the reverend while he's in mourning. One week and he will be talking business again. He must be the first to learn of it outside of my father and Edward, so we must keep it a secret until then."

Once again, she reminds me of my fate and my face falls.

"I'm sorry, ma'am." She rests a comforting hand on my arm, and I force a bright smile on my face.

"I'm happy for you, Goody. Really happy. You are the lucky one."

"I count my blessings, ma'am, and thank the good lord for granting me happiness."

I can't help hating every word she says because surely if the good lord had any hand in happiness, this town would be a very different place. Instead, I nod. "Well, I suppose we're all packed."

"I should go and prepare supper, ma'am."

"Of course. Thanks, Goody, you've been a great help."

As she leaves, I sit on my bed with only my troubled thoughts for company. Supper will be ready in two hours' time, after which I'm expected to leave my childhood home for my marital one. I picture it as my own last supper before my life changes forever.

It's as if we live in ancient times and I hate every minute of it. I am filled with despair because they have backed me into a corner, and I have nowhere to run. Not without Hope, anyway. More than anything, I am impatient to get to her because my baby is the only thing that matters above my own life. Knowing she is being held hostage in the reverend's home fires up my anger and causes the beast inside me to roar.

The door opens and I struggle to control my anger as mom heads inside and wastes no time in sitting beside me on the bed.

"What?" I say angrily and she says with disapproval. "Anger is the curse of the devil."

"Not from where I'm sitting."

"Faith!" she says with a warning in her voice, and I bite back.

"Why mom? This isn't right and you know it."

"It's the best for you and for Hope."

"And for you. You told me downstairs. You sold me out to get your reputation back and to *him*. How could you?"

The disgust is evident in my voice and to my surprise,

mom says in a sad voice. "I'm sorry, Faith, you have every right to be angry with us."

It shocks me silent because for the first time in my life, my mother is apologizing to me.

"I was young once, Faith."

I still as a little of mom's past unravels before me.

"I understand what it's like. What it's like to want something forbidden."

A hushed silence falls between us as she whispers, "I was always told not to look, but I did. Of course, I did. There was a boy who stared at me in class. I felt his eyes burning into me. Grady Montague. He had an energy none of the other boys had. His father was one of the wealthiest men in Heaven and he wore clothes we had never seen the like of before. Grady enjoyed an arrogance that I found intoxicating and I was fascinated by him."

I say nothing because I am enthralled by my mom's story because I never really saw her as a person until now. She has always just been mom, and I never imagined her life without my father in it.

Before she became his possession.

"One day I was walking home after class, and I dropped my books in a puddle. I was so scared, Faith."

She whispers, "I didn't know what to do. As I tried to gather them, a shadow fell over me and Grady dropped before me, and his hand rested on mine."

Her voice has changed, as if the memory is her most precious one and she whispers, "I looked up into two dark brown eyes and I have never seen the look of them before. They mesmerized me and I couldn't place the expression in them. His hand was warm, secure even, and as he leaned forward, I almost tasted his breath as he whispered, 'I will deal with this.' His hand grew tighter around mine and he pulled me closer, my face almost touching his and he told me he had his eye on me and would arrange our marriage as soon as we left school."

"What happened?" I'm almost afraid to ruin her story by reminding her I am here, but she shakes her head and carries on.

"I don't know how it happened, but he shifted closer. I should have pulled away, but he was in command of me. Our lips touched, and I felt a fluttering deep inside and then he pressed harder, and his tongue parted my lips and delved inside. I had never been kissed before and was frightened, but there was something preventing me from doing anything to ruin the moment." Her face flames with embarrassment as she whispers.

"We kissed in broad daylight on the path near the buttercup field and it was the most magical moment of my life."

"What happened?" I am almost afraid to ask because this was not a happily ever after for the two would-be lovers.

"He died."

"How?"

The desolation in her voice breaks my heart as she says sadly. "A riding accident. He came off and hit his head. He died in the hospital a few days later."

"I'm so sorry, mom."

She forces some brightness into her voice. "It was God's will. I was always to be married to your father, and I was destined to bring you into the world and so…" She turns and stares deep into my eyes with her apology evident. "Life doesn't always turn out how we want it to, but God sees the bigger picture. What happened to you was unfortunate, but this is your salvation. The reverend will make a fine husband and provide a good home for you and Hope. Just remember the good times are only of the moment. They never last and what's important is duty above fanciful ideas of love."

She says love. Was it ever love with Jonny? It certainly felt like that at the time, but distance has faded the memory of love. Lust definitely, but surely if I loved him, I wouldn't have run. Or is it because I loved him too much? I will never know because Jonny is gone and in his place is a man who stars in my nightmares and is my punishment, my damnation, and my future.

CHAPTER 6

JONNY

The town is exactly how I remember it. Nothing ever changes here. It's still the same boring town that I grew up in.

I park the bike outside the general store and note the turned gazes of the passers-by, desperate not to stare into the devil's eyes.

There are no friends to look up, no old teachers to revisit. I have no one but Faith, and even she turned her back on me. Why am I even bothering?

I head inside the general store and the chatter falls silent as my heavy boots make the floorboards creak. I wink at a couple of girls cowering in the corner and the flush on their faces makes me smile.

"Ladies." I say in my husky drawl and from out of nowhere their moms appear and hurry them away.

"Good to see you, Mr. Gaston." I say cheerily to the store-keeper, and he blinks as he recognizes one of their own.

"Is that you Jonny Santos?"

He stares at me, aghast, and I nod. "The same, although dressed a little differently now."

He runs his eyes over my biker jacket and, for some reason, a small smile tugs at his lips.

"Have you been home to see your folks?"

I lean over the counter and whisper, "It didn't go well."

"I'd be surprised if it had."

He whispers back, causing me to grin.

Mr. Gaston was always a diamond in the rough and, for some reason, held a soft spot for me. I could always score a few sweets from him when my mom's back was turned, and I enjoyed our chats when I used to help him with his deliveries. It's sad when my only friend in town is old enough to be my father, but I always thought of him more in that role than my own.

He jerks his head and calls to his wife. "Martha, I'm heading out back. Cover the counter."

Martha nods, a small smile on her face as she watches us go, and it strikes me that I feel more at home here than in my own. Martha was no different to Mr. Gaston and always slid a warm bun from the oven my way, or a mug of cocoa when I most needed it. I loved my time with them, and it was inevitably the next place to visit on my list.

"Take a seat, Jonny."

Mr. Gaston points to the faded couch and reaches for a bottle in the cupboard.

"Is that …?" I say in surprise, and he winks.

"I think you could use some."

I watch as he splashes a shot of whiskey into a glass and pours one for himself.

"To reunited friends." He raises his glass and I nod. "Friends."

We down the shot in one and he sits beside me and says in a low voice.

"We missed you, Jonny."

His words are unexpected and for some reason cause a

lump in my throat that I wasn't expecting. I can't even answer him, and he slaps me on the back and chuckles softly. "What's up? You lost the power of words, son?"

My eyes water as he calls me son because I always wished he was my own father. If I could choose anyone I would rather be raised by, its Mr. Gaston and his wife Martha. Two warm-hearted people who exist surrounded by souls of ice.

"Then you're the only one." I say with a hollow laugh, and he sighs heavily.

"You understand how it is here. This town is so steeped in the past, it has no room for progress."

"Why do you stay here?"

I'm curious and he shrugs. "I have Martha and my store. Business is good and we get by. Life isn't always greener on the other side, Jonny, when you have everything you want."

"Do you?" I stare around me at a relic from the past, picturing my own modern living that is several generations away from this one.

"I have love, Jonny. I have Martha, and everything else comes second to that."

"Then you're the lucky one."

He hesitates before he says with a guarded tone.

"There is something I think you should know, but before I mention it, why are you really here?"

"Unfinished business."

His deep sigh follows, and he groans. "I thought so."

"So, what do you want to tell me?"

I lean back and stare at him with interest, and it appears he is struggling to decide what words to use.

"Faith came back."

I say nothing, but my heart lurches at the mention of her name.

He carries on. "She needs you."

"Why? She didn't need me when she ran away from me. What's changed?"

"It's not for me to say." He looks worried. "I'm only telling you this because that little lady is in deep trouble, and I'm hoping you can help."

"Trouble." I lean forward, my eyes narrowing to dangerous slits.

"What, danger?"

"You didn't hear this from me, ok?"

"I promise, and you have my word on that."

He nods, a worried frown appearing on his usually agreeable face.

"She is to be married."

His words plunge that rusty knife in deeper and I hiss.

"Then I have nothing left to stay for."

He shakes his head. "You don't understand. She has been *told* she is getting married."

"I suppose that's how it works around here. Why should I care? She didn't want me."

My words are empty, but my heart is not. I am burning up inside, my emotions out of control because just the mention of her has the ability to bring me to my knees.

"Keep on telling yourself that and you will lose her."

I'm shocked at the venom in Mr. Gaston's words, and he says in an urgent whisper,

"Listen hard, Jonny. This is my gift to you. In ten days' time, Faith will be married off to Reverend Peters and he has told his congregation he will banish the devil from inside her. She is a project, a statement, and her life is about to get a whole lot worse. That man has just buried wife number four and you need to start asking questions about that. He hides behind the bible and preaches what the rest of them want to hear. He is corrupt, sadistic and the least holy person I've ever met, and someone needs to stop him. YOU need to stop him, Jonny. I have every faith in you."

Just the mention of his name causes my blood to boil because I know only too well what methods Reverend Peters uses on the wicked. My own parents sent me to him for salvation and I still bear the scars today of that sadistic freaking horror show. Just the idea of Faith anywhere near that bastard has my wolf howling and my claws sharpening.

Mr. Gaston says quickly, "I will help you, but it must not come at any cost to me."

I stare at him with acceptance because we're not talking money here. Mr. Gaston enjoys a relatively quiet existence in Heaven, and I must protect that at all costs.

He nods as he sees the determination in my eyes.

"There is a cabin in the woods, off the beaten trail. It's yours for the duration of your visit here. I will bring supplies up later, but nobody must discover I helped you."

"You can rely on me." I nod because he is speaking my language. Covert operations are what I excel at and I'm not a fool. I know his life would be over in this town if word got out, which is why, for everyone's sake, this mission must be a successful one.

CHAPTER 7

FAITH

I want to run so badly, but it's as if my feet are set in cement. We are standing in front of the house that may end my life. I'm not a fool. I know the shelf life of one of the reverend's wives isn't a long one, but I've been duped by the people who should have had my best interests at heart above their own.

Mom and dad stand close as if anticipating my escape and as the doorbell rings, I swallow hard.

Footsteps click on what must be a hard surface behind the heavy wooden door and I'm guessing there's not a lot of comfort to be had inside these four walls.

The door opens and my father growls, "Stand up straight, Faith. Do not let us down."

If I could kill anyone right now, it would be him because any love I ever had died the moment he sold me to a tyrant.

A patrician looking woman regards us through narrow slits and her pursed lips indicate her disapproval as she casts a malevolent gaze up and down my entire body.

"He's expecting you." She says in a voice devoid of

emotion and as we follow her inside, a shiver ripples through my entire body.

This place is already depressing, and we've only just stepped inside.

Stark walls decorated only with one solid wooden crucifix beckon me to damnation. The polished wooden floor gleams as we tread a dangerous path and the various doors set into the wall probably hide cold comfort if this is anything to go by.

She opens a door at the end of the narrow hallway and says politely, "Your visitors have arrived, sir."

We hear nothing, but she steps to one side and jerks her thumb into the room and as we head inside, my knees tremble when I see the man waiting for me.

He rises from behind a huge wooden desk in a room filled with leather-bound books. There is one solitary light and no window covering, and the only art on the wall is a picture of the last supper.

It is so cold in here and I shiver not only from terror but because he has the window open and if I could, I would dive headfirst through it because this is not a happy home. Far from it. It's a prison and I am in no doubt that I will pay a heavy price during my time here.

Reverend Peters completely ignores me and addresses my father. "Cyrus. Please take a seat."

He nods to the upright wooden chair set before his desk, and I stand beside my mom as if we are invisible to him. If only that were still the case.

"We have an agreement." The reverend says and still hasn't glanced once in either mine or mom's direction.

"For the next ten days, there will be no contact with your child."

Mom brushes her hand against mine and it shocks me a

little. After her story today, my heart has softened toward her and I brush mine back in a gesture of support.

My father merely nods, and the reverend says firmly, "She will remain here during the preparations of our wedding. At no time must you question my methods, knowing that everything I do is for the good of conquering evil. Do we have an agreement?"

Part of me hopes my father will stand up for once in his life, but my hopes are dashed when he says loudly, "We would be honored for you to take our daughter in hand, Reverend."

I make to speak, and mom nudges me as the men stand and shake hands across the table.

As he straightens up, the reverend says dismissively, "You may both leave."

Just like that, my parents fade from my side as if they were smoke. Quietly, no gestures, no emotion, and no goodbyes. The door shuts quietly behind them, and I stand awkwardly in the center of the room waiting for the ax to fall.

The reverend moves from behind the desk and stands facing me, some distance apart.

"Turn around." He commands and like a piece of cattle, I pirouette so he can assess his purchase.

As I face him again, he shakes his head.

"I have a lot of work to do."

He approaches me and hisses, "Kneel."

Once again, I foolishly open my mouth to speak, but before any words make it out, he strikes me hard across the face and yells. "I SAID KNEEL!"

I am so shocked I fall to the ground and tremble before him, as he places his hand on top of my head and says a prayer for my soul. My face is burning and not only from the pain because I am mortified to be in this position at all.

I try to focus on the one reason I am here and offer my own silent prayer to God to reunite me with my child and as soon as he finishes, he says in a curt voice with no emotion.

"You will be confined to your room. Miss. Hughes will bring you food and water and you have seven days to learn the bible in its entirety."

"My baby."

I foolishly blurt out and am rewarded with another slap across the face.

"Do not speak." He hisses and I try so hard to stem the tears that are bubbling up as he hisses, "Seven days to learn the bible. If you pass the test, I will allow you access to your bastard. Miss. Hughes will care for it and if you ever want to see it again, you will do as I say."

I'm shocked when his fingers filter through my hair and then he grabs it hard and pulls my head up to face him. The look on his face makes me weak with terror because this man isn't sane. He's mad.

His eyes flash with the power he has over me and the snarl on his face tells me I'm in trouble and, as he pulls down sharply, he growls, "Your hair will be the first thing to go. To drive the demon out, you need to be stripped back. A shaven head offers no vanity. A simple cotton tunic offers no attraction and a face devoid of paint gives the devil nothing to hide behind."

He pulls me roughly to my feet and I feel his breath against my face as he hisses, "I will break you, girl, and let those demons out. Only then will I rebuild you into the wife I deserve. To serve me, to be at my command and to satisfy my physical needs. You will have no voice, no control, and no life without me by your side and your bastard will be brought up to respect the lord and be obedient in our ways. The sins of the mother will not be bestowed on the child and so any claim you have has ended today. You are not fit to be a mother because you are an evil, filthy whore."

Once again, he strikes me hard three times around the face and as the blood from my nose splashes on the ground, it's quickly joined by my tears.

He steps away and rings a bell and almost immediately the door opens, and he says in a cold voice. "Show the whore to her room and lock her in."

Somehow, I find the strength to follow the silent woman dressed in black and sin, and she leads me up a wooden staircase to a room at the end of a bare hallway.

As she opens the door, silently and with a sneer on her lips, she slams it shut behind me and, as the key turns in the lock, I stare at my prison with a growing sense of desperation.

He wasn't kidding, this room is a prison because inside these four walls is nothing but walls, a mattress and a wooden table and chair and there on the center of the table is the biggest bible I have ever seen with one stark lightbulb hanging above it. A bucket in the corner is my only means of relieving myself and I have seven days to do the impossible.

CHAPTER 8

JONNY

One hour later, I have everything I need. The key to the cabin along with the directions.

I will be eternally grateful to Mr. Gaston because he has stepped out of his comfort zone to help a renegade and his real fear for Faith has hardened my resolve.

I head to my bike, ignoring the curious glances of the passers-by, intent on heading to Faith's parents' house and demanding to see her.

I know it won't go down well, but my rage knows no reasoning and yet as I reach my girl, I notice a white piece of paper tucked in the seat.

I waste no time in grabbing it and am intrigued by the words on the page.

Meet me at the Henderson barn

As I sit astride my bike, I wonder who could have sent the note. One of my parents, perhaps. Doubtful.

Definitely not the two people inside the store, so either someone has seen me, or word spreads fast around here.

My curiosity wins as always and I steer the bike toward the meeting place, hoping like crazy that it's Faith and I can tuck her behind me on the Harley and get the hell out of Heaven.

My hometown exists as the land that time forgot. Nobody comes here unless they have a connection to the town and visitors are as scarce as any humanity in this place. As a child, this is your world. There is nothing else and there isn't anyone around to tell you differently. No television, no radio, and no contact with the outside world. There were hushed words on the street about a different world far away, but nobody ever believed it. It was just a dream. The devil's work some said, but I was curious. That curiosity manifested itself into an idea that grew by the day, and as soon as I was old enough, I made my escape. One of the delivery trucks that rolled into town was the perfect wagon to carry me away. Not that the driver was aware of anything as I stowed away in his vehicle without his knowledge. It was a long trip, and I only had the water I brought with me and a small amount of food that I stole from our kitchen.

I had very little, and it angered me when I reached my destination and saw exactly what they had been hiding from us. Civilization.

I stepped from that truck into a world I never even knew existed. It blinded me. The world was amazing, beautiful, and extreme.

As I walked the streets, I stared in awe at the colorful shop windows, dodged the intense traffic and marveled at the houses that were far better than anything I had ever seen.

I was naive and trusting and learned the rules the hard way.

The first sign I saw advertising a job, I stepped inside to

apply. I had no social security number and no fixed address. I was nobody.

I felt like a fool.

I lived rough on the streets and opened my ears. Learning everything I could about this strange new world, and soon found myself on the doorstep of the military recruitment center where I found the place I belonged.

They arranged everything. My life became theirs as they made a citizen of me, and I was grateful for the opportunity. I learned my lessons well and bonded with my platoon and soon I was untouchable. My skill, as it happens, is killing. Fighting and strategic planning. I became good at what I did, and I was soon educated in more than war. The women who flocked around us when we hit the town were an education of the sweetest kind. I discovered a love of soft flesh and willing lips, stolen kisses, and gentle touches. I thought I had died and gone to my own version of heaven on earth, which revealed that my own town was built on a lie. Heaven isn't a place on earth and definitely not the one I came from. It's a different thing entirely.

I grew up in Heaven and became a man in the military, and I suppose I would still be there now if I hadn't gone home for a visit where my life took a new direction. I met Faith, which changed everything, but now as I approach the Henderson barn; I wonder if it had all been for nothing.

I park my bike some distance away and make the rest of the journey on foot. Surveillance was always one of my sharpened skills and so I take the route in through the forest that offers cover. I am silent, deadly and any compassion was left on the war-torn fields of distant lands and as I head closer, even the birds don't register my arrival.

The Henderson barn is a dilapidated structure that was left to nature when its owner died a horrific death farming one day. Amos Henderson was a recluse which killed him in the end. He trapped his foot in the plow and was dragged around his own fields until he was no longer living. The jackals found him before help and there were no friends or family to mourn his passing or inherit his farm. It became an open grave for the poor man who loved it and, as I approach, the creak from the open door is the only sound as it swings in the slight breeze.

Quietly, I head inside the darkened interior and, as my eyes adjust, a whisper from the darkness stops me in my tracks.

"Over here."

I peer into the gloom and am surprised to see the white cotton of a dress, revealing this is no threat to me, causing me to relax.

"Jonny."

For a moment my heart lifts, hoping like hell its Faith, but as she steps into the light, she reveals herself to be her best friend instead.

"Purity. Is that you?" I ask in my husky drawl, and she says with fear in her voice, "I shouldn't be here. Nobody must know."

She steps into the light, and I regard her ashen face, staring at me with a mixture of fear and relief.

"Thank the lord you came."

"What is it darlin'?" I say kindly and she peers nervously around her and whispers, "Faith. She's in danger."

"How?" My voice comes out like a rusty blade on a battle shield because there is no way in hell I'm leaving her here and Purity nods, the relief shining in her eyes as she whispers, "She is due to marry Reverend Peters in nine days' time. She would be signing her death warrant."

"So I've heard." I hiss and her eyes widen.

"We need to rescue her."

"Rescue?" I raise my eyes and she nods, peering around with wide-eyed fear.

"She is being kept prisoner until the day before her wedding. I overheard my father telling my mother."

"How does he know?" I'm curious and Purity says quickly, "He works for Reverend Peters. He cares for his business interests, and they have many meetings that I make a point of attending."

"They let you?" I'm surprised at that, and her impudent grin makes me smile because it appears that Purity Sanders is a girl after my own heart.

"*I* let me, Jonny. They don't even know I'm there."

She carries on quickly. "I want to help you, but nobody must ever discover my part in this."

Anonymity is a recurring theme in this town, so I nod. "Of course."

She moves closer and stares at me with the wide eyes of the innocent and says in awe, "What's it like, Jonny?"

"What?"

"Life outside this town. Is it really as bad as everyone says it is?"

"Of course not."

I shake my head. "This town fabricates stories to keep everyone here. If they realized what life was really like, they would pack up and move on in no time. Don't be afraid of what's out there, Purity. Be afraid of missing it."

"That's what Faith said."

"She left town?"

That would explain why I couldn't find her, and she nods. "She got as far as Jackson's point before they found her and brought her back."

"What happened?" The pain is unbearable knowing she ran from me, and Purity surprises me by placing a gentle hand on my arm. "Don't be angry, Jonny. You haven't heard the full story."

"Then tell me."

"I can't." She shakes her head.

"Only Faith can tell you, but it's obvious she still loves you. She always has, probably too much."

"What makes you say that?"

"She told me." Her simple answer knocks me out far more than any act of violence could. She loves me. Then why run? It doesn't make sense.

Purity drags my mind back to business and says with an urgency that doesn't escape me.

"She is locked up in the reverend's house. She has seven days before he lets her out of her room, and that is when her training begins."

"Her training?"

Purity nods. "I overheard him telling my father. She will be tested and if she passes, he will allow her to prepare for the wedding and married life with him."

"If she fails?" My voice is laden with animosity, and she shakes her head, looking worried. "He told my father he would break her and drag the devil out from inside her. My father asked how and then he laughed and said, the usual way a man breaks a woman. Her spirit, her body, and her humanity."

I clench my fists, knowing only too well how the reverend drags the demons out and my first instinct is to head over there right now.

I say roughly, "Like fuck will I wait. I'm getting her now and if anyone gets in my way, they will meet their lord a lot sooner than they think."

"No, Jonny! Stop!"

The fear in Purity's voice makes me stop and turn and I can tell there is piece of this puzzle I'm still searching for.

"Faith won't thank you for busting her out. You need to trust me and listen."

I fall silent as she says nervously, "I can get you in to see her, but she is locked in her room. You may be able to speak through the door and figure out a plan between you."

"You can get me in. How?"

I'm mildly curious and amused at the brave woman who looks as if she would have a heart attack if the wind blew in the wrong direction and her impudent smile makes me chuckle softly as she shrugs. "The reverend holds a service every second day at sunrise. The whole town attends, as I'm sure you remember. Well, that includes Miss. Hughes, so you will have one hour to head inside and speak to Faith."

I nod in agreement, but my heart is hurting so bad right now. Talk to Faith. Will it really be so easy and what happens when I see her again? It could change everything and nothing at the same time. I will finally discover why she ran from me and if I like what I hear, seven days is shit because she will be heading home with me that same night and we will never look back.

CHAPTER 9

FAITH

I have been reading the bible all day and the words blur under my tears as the stench of the bucket in the corner reminds me of how basic my life is now. If it only concerned me, I would never be here at all. I would have run, fought my way out of trouble and never looked back.

But they took the one thing that means everything to me in life and have hidden her away.

I know she's not here. I only came here for my baby, but it's obvious to me she is somewhere else. For the first hour of my incarceration, I listened for any sound of her at all. *There was none.* I thought she was asleep. That must be the case, but no. It's a feeling inside me that is impossible to ignore. My baby is no longer here, so where the hell is she?

I must have sat at the table for half a day before Miss. Hughes unlocks the door and I almost consider attacking her and running like hell. Her words banish that possibility when she sets the loaf of dry bread on the table alongside a pitcher of water.

"Your child is being cared for elsewhere."

"Where is she?" I scream at the wretched woman and

make toward her and I'm shocked when she pulls out a pistol and snarls. "Give me a reason to use this, whore."

I stop and she snarls, "You do not deserve the reverend's attention. He is a good man who is plagued by the restraints of forgiveness. Your bastard child has been sent away until your demons are conquered and if you ever want to see it again, you will do as he says and be thankful for it."

My verbal abuse hits the slamming door and I cry wretched tears of anguish that spill onto the pages of the bible. I have no choice but to see this through and until I discover where Hope is, and she is safe in my arms, I will do as I'm told.

It's difficult to sleep with pain driving deep inside me. There is an empty space where my heart used to be. I try not to think of Hope. I try not to think of Jonny. I only try to think of a way out of this horror show.

* * *

SOMEHOW, I fall asleep, only to wake when I am dragged from my mattress by my hair and forced into the wooden chair, the single light bulb shining in my eyes.

"What's happening?" I gasp as I am tied to the chair with a rope.

My heart lurches in fear as Reverend Peters steps into view and I try not to stare at his evil face as he peers at me with a slightly crazed expression in his eyes.

"Blessed is the man that walketh not in the counsel of the ungodly, nor standeth in the way of sinners, nor sitteth in the seat of the scornful." He says with a hiss.

"But his delight is in the law of the LORD; and in his law doth he meditate day and night."

He snaps, "What is the psalm I recite?"

My mind struggles to focus as I think back on what I

read, but the panic inside me is controlling me right now and I sob. "I don't know."

He strikes me hard around the face and the tears splash down my cheeks, no longer able to stay hidden.

"How can I be happy in this life?"

He says roughly. "That is the meaning of the first psalm of the bible, and you must raise that question every day of your life. Let me tell you what that means for you."

I say nothing and hate how my face burns as he sneers, "Happiness to you is serving me. If I am happy, you are happy. If I smile, you smile. If I sleep, you sleep. Do I make myself clear?"

"Yes." He strikes me again, causing me to scream, and he roars, "YES, SIR!"

"Yes, sir."

I sob as he starts to pace the small room.

"You must renounce evil. Turn your back on sinners and pledge undying love to the lord."

"Yes, sir."

I am saying whatever he wants to hear because I am in no position to make a stand.

"Let me make this clear, whore."

He snarls, dropping down before me and grabbing my smarting face with his hands, causing me to wince at the pain.

"I am your lord. You will serve me and if you don't measure up, you will be punished."

He squeezes hard and I almost believe he will break my jaw as his eyes burn into mine with an intensity that scares the shit out of me. He is something else. Mad, crazy and dangerous and I can't fight against one of them, let alone all three.

"Tonight, I will teach you. You will learn from your master and tomorrow you will return to the bible and memorize every word. Every night I will return and if you fail my test, your punishment increases. Do I make myself clear?"

"Yes, sir." I gasp through the pain, and he releases my face and grabs my hair in a strong grip, pulling down hard on it, causing me to scream in pain.

"The day after our wedding, you will lose this monstrosity. You will be required to wear a bonnet in public, and no man will ever look at you again. *I* will try not to look at you because you have the eyes of a witch. I will use your body for my own pleasure and to plant my seed, and you will spread your legs for no other man. You have committed the ultimate sin and will endure your punishment in penance for them. Only then will I allow you to see your child. Only when I am assured you will not corrupt another innocent soul, and only when I am certain your bastard has not inherited your wantonness."

I long to ask after my daughter. I am crazy with fear for her. This is a nightmare I can see no way out of because they are using the one weapon against me that will win them this war.

Hope.

CHAPTER 10

JONNY

The frustration is tearing me up inside. When Purity left, I waited one hour before making my way to the cabin Mr. Gaston provided and, as I turn the key, I am emotional when I see the supplies resting on the scrubbed wooden table. His kindness means more than he will ever know because inside this town, I haven't received much of it.

I fix myself a plate of eggs, bacon, and fried potatoes and as I sit, I consider my options.

My entire focus is on only one thing. Faith. There is something I'm not seeing. Something that has lit the fear of God in the eyes of Purity and Mr. Gaston. Something they can't speak of, and the answer lies with only one person.

Just picturing her face fills me with a longing I tried so hard to erase as I searched for release inside the whores I fucked. She never went away, and I felt as if I betrayed her every single fucking time, but I needed to get her out of my system.

It was impossible.

I volunteered for every mission and every trip just to distance my mind from her, and I even went undercover with the mafia just to eradicate her from my memory.

None of it worked, and when Ryder insisted I return home to see my folks, I thought he was an interfering bastard. Now I'm not so sure that was the real reason for my visit at all.

I type out a text to the man himself to search for my own set of answers.

JONNY

Find out what you can about Reverend Peters. He has buried four wives, which is either extremely unfortunate or extremely careless.

I throw down my cell and am grateful for the cold beer Mr. Gaston has provided despite the fact alcohol is strictly limited to the dens of the men in this town.

It's always been the same here. The men rule and the women accept it. Men drink, do business and have their freedom. Women have none of the above. Now I understand what real life involves it makes me even madder and the longer I spend around these people the likelier I am to snap.

Technology hasn't caught up with Heaven and they live like puritans and all because of the church. It's almost a cult, and I wonder why the authorities never stepped in. It's a mystery that has the Twisted Reapers' name all over it, which once again raises the question why I was persuaded to come here at all.

Two hours later, I receive a text from Ryder.

RYDER

I've put Brewer and Lucy on it. Tread carefully and if you need backup, we require a day's warning, or I can send a crew now.

JONNY

A day!

I type back with a smile and get the response I wanted by return.

RYDER

I'm not God, Sinner. Even I need to arrange a flight to the middle of god-damned nowhere.

Sinner. It makes me smile because when they learned of my mom's parting words to me, the name kind of stuck and they call me it more for their own amusement than a reason. I am Sinner of The Twisted Reapers MC, and I'm a bad-assed motherfucker who gives zero shits. At least that's what I tell everyone, but in unguarded moments like this, I am only fooling myself. I give too many shits and they all involve one tiny woman who grabbed my heart and ran away with it.

Tomorrow, I will see her again and despite what Purity thinks, I *will* be seeing her. There will be none of this locked door shit because nothing on this earth will stop me from seeing my woman, whether she agrees with that title or not.

* * *

AFTER THE MOST frustrating twenty-four hours of my life, I am holed up out of sight in the bushes surrounding Reverend Peter's home. I got here early and settled down for a reconnaissance mission that must be a success.

I observe the reverend going about his business, followed closely by the dour old witch Miss. Hughes. The way she scurries around after him tells me everything I need to know. She loves him. Idolizes him even and for a dried-up old spinster like her, it must be painful watching him take wife number five, knowing she is never in the running.

Nobody visits the Peter's home and I expect it's because technically he's still in mourning. I stare with anger as he steps onto the porch, a tall thin figure dressed in a cheap black suit that hangs off him as if it's repulsed to even touch him. His thinning hair is combed over the bald spot on his head, and his shifty eyes glance around furtively as he taps his foot on the wooden boards. He is holding a bible in his right hand and his black gloves in the other and the pallor of his skin makes his sunken eyes appear quite monstrous.

Reverend Peters is a fucking joke and I long to end his life with one well-aimed bullet from my gun.

I could do it. I *should* do it and save us all a whole lot of misery. I wouldn't be prosecuted. I've killed more prominent men than him, but it needs to be a direct order from my president, rather than an act of malice on my behalf.

Perhaps that will be my next text. To seek permission to send the bastard to meet his dead wives, although I'm guessing they have discovered where Heaven really is, and the bad reverend's destination will be a far hotter one.

He glances at his wristwatch and as the door opens, I note his trusted servant step beside him in a floor length dress with a cape around her shoulders. She is wearing a felt hat and I want to laugh out loud because what century do these fucking people live in?

This is their life; their world and modern living never made it this far. They work hard on the land providing a meager existence and I wonder why they don't chance their luck anywhere else.

Once again, I think back on my own childhood and realize the people are brainwashed into believing this is what life offers. It's only when someone steps outside and takes a chance, they see it's definitely not the case. They never come back because why would they? Until now, of course. Until a Reaper came to town.

* * *

THEY FINALLY LEAVE and set off in the small black car like two actors in a Netflix documentary. As soon as the car disappears from view, I head toward the house, my heart beating so fast I may not make it.

As I edge open the door, I smile to myself. Foolish mistake, although I'm guessing he expects everyone to be waiting in his church. They wouldn't dare not show up, which makes this easy for me.

They think I've gone. Left already because that is what Mr. Gaston has promised to leak around town. I make interesting gossip in the store, and I have a willing companion who would help spread the lie. I drove to the county line and then doubled back cross country to the mountain where Mr. Gaston has his bolthole. Mainly as a place to shoot and fish high above the plains of Heaven, but the perfect place for me to sharpen my resolve.

The house is in silence and as I tread the wooden staircase, the boards creak under the weight of my boot. My heart hammers and the sweat builds as I anticipate a meeting that is long overdue.

I listen for any signs of life and only the gentle sobs of an angel reveal my destination and my heart hardens as I make my way to the door at the end.

CHAPTER 11

FAITH

*I*t's only when I'm sure they left, do I give in to my grief. I sit on the mattress and draw my knees to my chest and let emotion have its day. Five more days of hell to endure before what? Marriage to a bastard. The pain of not being with my child is tearing me apart, and even when that door is unlocked, I am not guaranteed to see her again. There are *no* guarantees, and I am crying because I can't figure a way of this fucking mess. The only thing I can think of is that one day I will take her and run. That is a given, but how long before I get the chance? Days, weeks, months, and God forbid years. I won't stay here forever, but it still *feels* like forever.

Suddenly, I'm aware of a noise at the door, a scraping on wood. Is it an animal, rats even? I wouldn't be surprised and I still as I strain to listen. It's a gentle scraping sound that tells me something is there, and I peer around me nervously because I have nowhere to hide. Surely, he didn't return. Is it Miss. Hughes, but she has a key? It must be a stranger or an animal.

I stare with a mixture of horror and a weird fascination as

the door handle turns and as the heavy door opens, I conclude I must be dreaming.

I blink in astonishment as the man I have tried so hard to forget stands in the doorway and I can't help the tears that splash down my face as I stare at what must be a hallucination.

"Are you real?" I blink several times to test the theory, and his low rumble of laughter makes me stare at him in surprise.

I'm not sure what's happening here because my eyes may not believe what's in front of them, but my heart obviously does.

"Jonny." My voice trembles and in two strides he is before me and pulling me into his insanely ripped arms. As they fold around me, I crumble. I can't help it as I sob like crazy on the shoulder of the man I have never stopped loving and as those arms fold around me, they bring with them the greatest sense of relief I have ever experienced in my life.

He nuzzles his face in my hair and whispers, "Don't cry, darlin', it's over."

I pull back and stare hungrily at a face I have tried so damned hard to forget and note the glittering dark eyes and the rough edges that surround raw beauty and the gentle smile of a sinner. His short dark hair is slightly long on top and the scuff on his jaw creates a hard edge to the person I know as anything but. Not with me, never with me, which is why it was so hard to walk away.

Tentatively, I reach up to test if he's real and, as my finger connects with his skin, his own hand lies against mine and he whispers, "What the fuck has he done to you?"

He gently traces the smarting skin that was so brutally beaten, and I whisper, "It's not so bad."

"I'll fucking kill the bastard." His ominous tone makes me smile because Jonny may be a sinner to most, but to me is everything. A gentle giant with the softest heart and the most caring lover. I feel safe with him. I always did.

"Why, Faith?"

I can tell he's hurting, although desperately trying hard not to show it and my voice shakes as I whisper, "I had no choice."

For a second, I witness the pain in his eyes, and it catches me deep in the heart and tears away another shred of my humanity because I put it there. He makes to speak, but I shake my head and with glistening tears in my eyes, I lean forward and press my lips to his with a deep sense of relief inside.

It's like coming home.

The memories dance around me, clapping their hands with joy because this is my happy place. In Jonny's arms, just the two of us. He pulls me in deeper and as his tongue edges inside, I feel the lit spark of chemistry we always had. It becomes the most important thing in life to savor this moment. Then again, it always was. He was an aching need inside me, a desire for something so perfect I would have done anything to take it. A hunger mixed with desperation for something so pure and my entire body trembles as we lose ourselves in perfection.

This kiss is not sexual, it's a homecoming and reminds me too well of what I walked away from. But it's not only me anymore and I can't be selfish, so I pull back and with glistening tears in my eyes, whisper, "There's something you should know."

I swear the tension increases in the room as he says gently, "You can tell me when we reach the cabin."

"The cabin?" I'm confused, and he strokes my face with a light touch and whispers, "There is no fucking way I'm leaving you here. There's a cabin in the wood we can hide out in tonight and then tomorrow I'm taking you away from this hellish place forever."

My eyes fill as the panic grips me and I shake my head and say quickly, "No!"

It's as if I've stabbed him several times over as the pain flares in his eyes and the rejection drives a wedge between us. He steps back a little and says in a hurt voice, "Why?"

My heart is beating so frantically I can almost hear it as I prepare to reveal to him something that may well finish the job and destroy him for ever.

"I can't leave."

"I don't understand."

My voice shakes as I whisper, "I want to leave with you so badly, Jonny. Trust me, I never meant to run. You were everything to me, but I had no choice."

"What do you mean, you had no choice? Of course you did. I would have cared for you, darlin', you know I would."

The tears spill down my face and I note the suspicion in his eyes as I prepare to deliver a life-changing moment.

"I have always known I'm safe with you, but it wasn't about me anymore."

"I don't understand?"

He appears genuinely confused and so, with a deep breath, I hold on to both his hands and say gently, "I ran because it wasn't just me." My voice breaks as I whisper, "We have a daughter, Jonny, and that is why I can't leave with you."

It's as if I've physically slapped him and he stares into my eyes with an expression of shock that tells me everything. I make to pull away and he grips me hard and says in a voice laced with pain, "I have a daughter."

"We do." I nod, my heart cracking under the pressure.

"Where is she?" He says with an urgency in his voice that

makes me crumble and the tears flow down my face as I sob, "I don't know."

"Then tell me what you *do* know." He says angrily and my voice rises as I say fearfully, "They took her when I was at the reverend's wife's funeral. I came home, and they told me I was going to become the reverend's wife number five and Hope was already with him."

"Hope." Jonny's eyes are wide, and I nod, feeling like the biggest bitch that ever existed.

"I called her Hope because that is what she meant to me."

"So, she's here. In this house." Jonny says, making to leave and I say quickly, "No. That is why I can't leave, because my only chance of ever seeing her again is by marrying that bastard. He told me I won't see her again until he has dragged the devil from inside me and he will raise her in the ways of Heaven. I'm scared, Jonny. He has my – our baby and I'm going out of mind."

For a second, he stands staring at me in shock as if he can't understand what I'm telling him and I say with a sob, "I'm so sorry, Jonny. I really am."

"Sorry!"

He shakes his head. "Sorry doesn't cut it, darlin'. You ran away from me knowing you were carrying my baby and you didn't think I'd be interested. You didn't trust me, Faith, and I'm finding it very hard to deal with that."

He looks so wounded I want to run to him and make everything better, but I know I can't. I doubt it will ever be better again and that's because of me, because of what I've done. I've wounded him so deeply he's struggling on life support right now and so I inject some steel into my voice and say quickly, "They can't find you here. You must lock me back in and let me do everything I can to get our baby back."

Jonny appears to shake himself and I watch the grim determination of a bastard settle over his face like a shield and for some reason, it freezes my blood. Now I see why he deserves his name because the man standing in the doorway deserves every syllable of it. They call him a sinner, well that makes two of us and for some reason his brutality gives me strength as he says in icy rage, "I'm going to get our baby back. Trust me, darlin', that bastard is a dead man walking."

"How?"

I'm both fearful and hopeful at the same time and he hisses, "Trust me, Faith. For once in your fucking life, trust me to do the right thing."

He stares at me with a hard expression. "As much as it kills me inside, you're right. You must stay here until I have our baby. Then I'm coming for you and this time you will *not* walk away from me. We will talk and figure things out and there will be no running this time. We will walk proudly away as a family and never step foot in this fucking pit again."

"Where will we go, Jonny?" I'm almost afraid to ask because the thought of life outside Heaven is scaring the pants off me.

"Hell, baby. I'm taking you to Hell and you will love every fucking second of it."

He turns to go, and I battle the pain knowing he is leaving because above everything I love this man so hard it physically hurts. Then he turns and in two strides pulls me roughly into his arms and kisses me so fiercely the spark between us explodes as it always did. Desire consumes me as we kiss like starving lovers and my body comes alive at the merest touch. Jonny equals passion and you don't get one without the other and as he pulls away, he stares deeply into my eyes and says huskily, "Trust me, Faith. That's all I ask."

He tears away from me and slams the door behind him, the sound of the lock jangling as he somehow locks me in again.

My tears fall like rapids as I hear his heavy boots walking away down the oppressive hallway and my body still burns from his touch.

My parents called him The Devil. Satan's soldier and now I know why. The image on his back as he walked away made my soul cower in fear. The Grim Reaper stared back at me with a grin and a promise, and it's obvious that when he left Heaven, Jonny walked straight into Hell.

CHAPTER 12

JONNY

*J*have never experienced pain like this. Somehow, I walked away from her. The woman who betrayed me. Ran away rather than face me with her secret and thought it better to be away from me than to face it together. It hurts like crazy, but feelings don't die easy and when I saw her again, every single fucking reason why I love this woman so hard came back with a vengeance. I will kill for Faith and I'm planning how to make it long, slow, and painful. That bastard ruined my life; is about to ruin Faith's life, but sure as I live and breathe, will not ruin my fucking daughter's life.

My daughter.

That word shocked me into being a man. I haven't even met her yet, but I already love her unconditionally. How could I not? She is formed from two people who explode worlds and after seeing Faith again, she is so deep inside my soul she will never escape. She is *my* woman, and I am her man. It was obvious from the moment I met her and despite everything, that feeling is still there standing in full sight, telling me I must do right by her.

I am angry, so fucking angry with her, the reverend and

this fucking town. I want to burn it up in my anger and tear it down, but only one thing is stopping me. My daughter. Hope.

Such a pretty name for an undoubtedly pretty girl. An innocent born into madness and where I intend on taking them isn't much better. I don't live a normal life. I never did, but if Faith believes I'm leaving them behind, then she's got another fucking thing coming.

* * *

I HEAD BACK to the cabin to plan my revenge, and it's burning me up inside. My fury is intense, and I want to smash something so badly. Anything but give into the pain of knowing my family is under siege. It goes against everything I've trained for to leave her behind, but that bastard mustn't know because the fate of my daughter is in his sadistic hands.

I pace the cabin floor, my mind veering out of control as I think up ways to kill the evil reverend. I'm not in control of my sanity right now and it's only when I catch sight of my reflection in the window, I remember who I am.

I am better than this.

I'm a trained operative with a sharp set of skills that will help me. Second to that, and probably even more important, I am not alone.

I reach for my cell and make the call, knowing I can rely on my brothers for help.

Ryder answers immediately.

"What's the matter? Missing us already?"

His low chuckle changes as I snap.

"I need your help."

"Go on."

His tone changes to bastard, which is exactly what I need, and I growl, "Turns out I have a daughter."

I stop because just saying that causes a sharp pain in my heart, knowing I've never even met her and she's in danger.

"Congratulations, Jonny."

Ryder's tone softens as he calls me by my real name for a change, and if anyone knows how I'm feeling now, it's the man who has a daughter of his own.

"She's been taken."

The silence on the other end tells me he's listening, and I snap, "Reverend Peters has hidden her somewhere and locked her mother in a room that is more like a prison. She is to marry him in a few days' time, and only then will he return our daughter if she passes some kind of fucked-up test."

"Fuck. I hate that shit."

Ryder growls because, like every Reaper in the compound, he hates anything to do with hurting women or children.

"I need to find out where she is before I rescue her mother. He can't know we're onto him because he could move Hope and we'd never see her again, or worse."

My voice catches and I'm surprised when Ryder's tone softens and he whispers, *"That's a pretty name, soldier."*

"It is."

My voice cracks and he says in a harder voice, *"Then remember your training. She needs a strong daddy now, and we must wrap this up quickly."*

"Yes, sir."

I shake myself and he says roughly, *"I want names of everyone connected to the reverend. I'll get Brewer onto it. Carry out your own surveillance and monitor every move that bastard makes. What about the law?"*

"There is none."

"No cops?"

He sounds disbelieving and I say roughly, "There is no

crime in Heaven. Not in plain sight, anyway. The cops aren't needed because the reverend runs the town, and the folks are so fearful they wouldn't even take a piss if he declared it sinful."

"Fuck me. Now I know why you left. Leave it with me. I'll drop a word in a few ears and get that town dragged back into the current century."

"After we find Hope."

I remind him and he growls, *"We will find your daughter, soldier, and that's a fact."*

I nod even though he can't see me because if I'm sure of anything, it's that.

He says with a heavy sigh. *"Leave it with me. I'll do some digging. Meanwhile, send me those names. Just say the word and we'll be there."*

"Thanks, Ryder."

"It will be my pleasure, soldier. Just remember your training and park emotion. It won't help the situation."

"I know."

He cuts the call and if anything, I am reassured that I'm not on my own anymore. I have two friends here who want to help, and a shit load of friends back in Washington. As it turns out, I also have a family right here in Heaven and as soon as we get the hell out of here, I'm going to be the best father I can and if Faith agrees, the best husband, too.

CHAPTER 13

FAITH

*M*y heart is still beating so fast, I wonder if it will ever slow down to a normal pace.

Jonny came for me.

When he walked into the room, my world stopped spinning while I stared at the man I have done everything to protect.

We met when he was home after leaving the military. I knew of him; hell, the whole town knew of Jonny Santos. He was a renegade even as a small child, and I was warned against him from a very young age. 'Don't look the devil in the eye' they told me and so whenever he was near, I cast my eyes to the floor.

Not that he ever looked at me. I was a child, a small girl, and yet he fascinated me. He had an aura surrounding him that I couldn't place. Confidence with a swagger that stuck two fingers up at the establishment. There was talk he was sent to Reverend Peters to have the devil dragged out from his soul. His hold was too strong because apparently, it never worked. When he finished school he left town, and I felt a strange emptiness when I heard the hushed whispers that the devil had dragged him to hell.

Life wasn't as exciting when he left and then a few years later, I bumped into him outside the general store one day.

I turned and ran into a wall of muscle and as my basket dropped to the floor, he bent down at the same time, and we knocked heads.

I will never forget the look he gave me when I stared into his dark brown eyes. It made my breath hitch and question my morality because I had never seen eyes gaze at me like that.

His strong hand covered mine and his husky voice told me he was sorry and to let him help me. A thousand emotions ran through me in a split second and something told me my life would never be the same again after Jonny.

I was right.

I hear the door slam and my heart starts thumping for a different reason entirely as I scoot to the chair and open the bible at the marker. I try desperately to read the blurred words as the footsteps make their way up the wooden steps and stop outside my door.

The sound of the lock turning makes me want to scream and as the reverend heads inside, he closes the door behind him.

"Kneel, whore."

He states in a harsh whisper, and I scrape back my chair and do as he says.

As always, he stops in front of me and places his hand on my head, uttering a prayer for my soul. Then he says brusquely, "Sit."

I react quickly and scurry to the chair and he stares at me long and hard and says angrily,

"A whore is a bottomless pit; a loose woman can get you

in deep trouble fast. She'll take you for all you've got; she's worse than a pack of thieves."

I say nothing and he barks. "Name the proverb."

I begin to shake. "I can't."

Once again, he steps forward and slaps me hard around the face, causing me to cry out.

"Proverbs 23:27-35."

He yells, "Say it!"

I struggle to remember what he even said and as I hesitate, he slaps me again so hard I fall off the chair to the wooden floor.

I'm shocked when he throws the pitcher of water over me and leans down, grabbing my hair as he yells, "I will drive the devil from inside you, whore. You will not steal from me."

"I don't understand." I'm foolish to even speak because he grips my face hard and his eyes flash as he hisses, "Do not speak unless asked a direct question. You will be punished for that."

He violently pushes me toward the table and forces me roughly down, face first and holding my neck with one hand, lifts my dress with the other, ripping down my panties with an angry growl. I tense in disbelief as he rains hard blows with his hand on my ass, causing me to cry out in pain. It only increases his anger, and the blows are harder, even more painful as they hit the already damaged skin. It's immeasurable agony and I choke on my sobs as he punishes me so severely, I doubt I'll be able to sit on the chair for a week.

Then he pulls me off the table and throws me down hard on the mattress, winding me slightly and wincing from the pain of his punishment, and he roars, "You have learned nothing. You are a useless piece of trash who is unfit to be a mother."

My blood runs cold as he sneers, "Your bastard child is better off without you. You have just days to learn the bible and if you don't quote every word at my request, your child will be sent away forever."

"No!" I yell, my pain forgotten as I find strength from somewhere and as he stares at me with cold derision, I do something I doubt either of us was expecting, and I fall to my knees and clench my hands together. "Please, sir. I'm begging you. Please don't send my daughter away. I, well, I love her with all my heart, and I will do anything to bring her back to me."

He stares at me with a blank expression, but his silence tells me I've surprised him.

For a moment, he says nothing at all as I bow my head and whisper, "Please, sir. I'll do everything you say. Just give me my baby back."

A shiver passes through me as he whispers, "She also lieth in wait as for a prey, and increaseth the transgressors among men."

I haven't a clue what he's talking about and as he starts pacing the room, I start to shiver.

He is mumbling almost to himself, as if he is arguing with his own mind, and then he stops and says in a strangely eerie voice, "Come with me."

I don't hesitate and stand as he leaves the room, expecting me to follow. My heart is thumping so hard because I am free for a moment. Free of the room and possibly free of the task he set me.

He leads me to a door set three doors away and as he enters, my heart almost gives out on me when I see we're in his bedroom. A wooden bed is the only large object in the room with a simple wooden table set beside it with the bible placed on the polished surface.

There is another door that must lead to his closet, and he says with a strange tone to his voice, "No temptation has overtaken you that is not common to man. God is faithful,

75

and he will not let you be tempted beyond your ability, but with the temptation he will also provide the way of escape, that you may be able to endure it."

I don't know what the hell is happening right now, and he opens the door and I see a small cupboard with nothing inside. It's effectively a wooden box.

"Get inside." He says roughly and I start to back away, shaking my head. "No."

His hand reaches out and snaps around my wrist and he says cruelly, "I will not be tempted by you, whore. My punishment for temptation is to lie with you away from my sinful touch."

He sneers, "You will spend the night in your prison as a punishment for trying to tempt me. I will be strong; I'll know you are close, but I must resist. It will be my penance for wicked thoughts. My test."

I struggle as he pushes me inside the confined space and scream as he slams the door shut and slides a bolt in place. I can see him through the latticed front and his cruel face leans against the panel and he whispers with a ragged breath, "You will not be my temptation, whore."

"Please. I'm begging you, don't do this."

I whisper, trying so hard not to crumble and he slams his fist against the wood and yells, "Enough!"

He steps away from the door, and I watch him pace around the room, muttering to himself and then to my horror, he wrenches off his clothes and stands naked in the center of the room.

"Is this what you want Lord?" He yells, holding out his arms. "Are you testing me?"

I am so shocked I fall silent as I stare in disbelief at a man who lost his sanity somewhere down the line.

He falls to his knees and sobs, before wailing like a child, and then he starts to pray in low murmurs of madness.

I have never seen anything like this before and it shocks me into silence. It *scares* me into silence, and it drives even more fear into my heart. Anything could happen with this man, and I may not make it to the wedding if the crazy takes over and so I shut my eyes, more out of self-preservation than anything and struggle to empty my mind of the horror show I am currently starring in the lead role.

CHAPTER 14

JONNY

I have a visitor. I am woken by the sound of tires on the woodland floor and jumping from my bed, I pull on my jeans and grab a t-shirt.

I head to the window and see Mr. Gaston hauling a crate of supplies from his truck and I breathe a sigh of relief.

As I head out to meet him, he says with concern. "You look like shit."

It makes me laugh. "Since when did you curse, Mr. Gaston?"

He grins. "Call me Arthur, Jonny. We are friends now."

His words mean more to me than he will ever know, and I say with a slight catch to my voice, "We are."

He grins as he thrusts the crate into my arms and says quickly, "Friends who breakfast together. I provided the food now you can cook."

I nod and head inside his small kitchen and place the crate on the counter and as I pull the ingredients out, he takes a seat at the table and says with interest, "How are things?"

"Not good, Mr. ...um, Arthur."

I sigh heavily. "It turns out I'm a father."

He looks startled. "Who told you that?"

"Faith." I shrug, knowing I can trust him, and he says incredulously, "You saw her?"

"Yes. I paid her a visit when the town was at Church. That bastard has her locked in a room with nothing but the bible."

Arthur shakes his head. "I knew she was in trouble."

He peers at me with concern.

"What about you? Are you in trouble, Jonny?"

His kind expression is exactly what I need right now, and I say with a deep sigh. "I think I am."

He says gently, "Then it's important we bring this to a close."

He reminds me what's important now and I push aside my own emotions and say quickly, "Do you know where my daughter is?"

"She's not there?"

He appears surprised and I hiss, "No. That bastard has sent her somewhere and is using her to break Faith. I need to find out where she is and who with. Do you have any ideas?"

"Boil the kettle, son, and I'll think on it."

He appears thoughtful, so I do as he says, grateful for the distraction. He remains silent as I busy myself preparing breakfast and only when I set two plates of eggs, bacon, hash browns and beans on the table, with two steaming mugs of coffee, does he speak.

"Augusta Hughes has a sister, Rosemary."

"The reverend's housekeeper, Miss Hughes?"

I can see where he's heading, and he nods, spearing a forkful of food and chewing it thoughtfully.

"She lives in Brindley Ridge, the next town over."

"I never knew she had a sister."

Come to think of it, why would I and Arthur nods. "She left a while back when their mom died. She is a teacher and went to work in the school there. Apparently, she fell in love with the place and set up home there permanently. She's never married though, and I'm guessing is the perfect person to care for a small baby."

"You could be right."

I reach for my cell and dash out a text to Brewer, before saying with a hard edge to my voice.

"Then I know where I'm going today."

"Is that wise?" He says with an arched brow.

"It's very wise." I bite back, and he shakes his head slowly.

"Listen, Jonny, the minute you ride in there, she will be on the phone to her sister before you can park the bike. Then what will you do? Take your daughter and get her to ride shotgun. She's a baby and they don't hang on very well."

His amused grin almost makes me laugh and I say wearily, "What do you suggest?"

He taps his finger on the table and says sternly, "You're a military man. Plan the operation."

Once again, somebody reminds me of my training and I'm grateful for it.

"Thanks, Arthur."

I sigh and slump back in my seat. "You're right, as always."

I grin as I lift the mug to my lips and start to form a plan in my head.

Arthur says carefully, "You will need help."

"What do you have in mind?"

"You may be good, Jonny, but you have a town against you. Those people may appear docile and subservient, but they're not against grabbing a shotgun or a pitchfork to defend their way of life. You go in all guns blazing and you'll have fifty more trained on you. The reverend has done an excellent job of brainwashing them, so you need to be smart about this."

He stops and fixes me with a hard stare. "Then there's Faith."

At the mention of her name, my heart lurches because seeing her yesterday was a blow to it that I'm still recovering from.

"What about her?" I say carefully.

"What are your intentions toward that poor girl?"

He appears almost fierce, and it makes me smile.

"I love her." The words leave my mouth before I can stop them and he appears happy about that and smiles, his eyes twinkling in the daylight.

"Then I have every answer I need. So, here's the plan."

For the next hour we discuss the operation that will bring my family back to me and now I have a mission, emotion is firmly checked and placed inside its box. The soldier in me takes over and I operate as a machine because, as it now happens, this will be the fight of my life and losing is definitely not an option.

CHAPTER 15

FAITH

I don't believe I slept all night. My heart almost gave out on me a few times when Reverend Peters prowled across to the cupboard and pressed his face to the lattice door. His rancid breath filled my space and his eyes probed into the darkness, flashing with pure evil.

He remained naked and moved around the room like a pacing lion, mumbling under his breath about resisting temptation and delivering him from evil.

The only thing keeping me going was the thought of Hope and Jonny. I must stay strong for them because I am confident that Jonny will make this nightmare go away.

My eyes fill with tears when I think about the man who crashed into my life so unexpectedly, not once, but twice. He is a force of nature, a thing of great beauty and so desirable I can't think straight when he's around.

As I cast my mind back to the day I discovered I was pregnant, I can still feel the fear inside me that cost me my rationality. I have been brought up to fear God and my parents in that order and I knew they would be angry, mortified, and publicly humiliated. It's why I ran, rather than face them, but the reason I ran from Jonny was a different one entirely.

I could never fear Jonny. I fear *for* him. He didn't need a child to worry about when he was due to return to active duty. He could lose his life at any moment, and it was easier to run than to say goodbye.

I was a fool. When I saw him again, I realized how important he is to me. Surely, any time with him is worth a lifetime of tears rather than regret. Then there's Hope. I denied them both and I feel like a fool as I blame myself for getting us all into this mess.

When I shut my eyes, I picture us a family, happy and laughing as families should. Not this. Not this existence. Life isn't living in Heaven. It's waiting to die.

I must fall asleep because as soon as the door opens, I tumble forward and only just prevent myself from falling onto the hard wooden floor.

The reverend is dressed, thank God, and he catches my arm and hisses, "Return to your studies."

I am glad to be away from him and scurry there quickly, noting the dry piece of bread and pitcher of water waiting on the table.

The door slams behind me and the lock is turned and the first place I head is to the bucket in the corner to relieve myself. I am degraded, scared and broken-hearted because every minute away from my baby is killing me inside.

Two days pass and I am buckling under the weight of it all. Miss. Hughes brings me the tiniest amount of bread and water and the evenings are spent being tested by Reverend Peters.

I always fail. It's an impossible task and the only thing keeping me going is knowing that Jonny is close and doing everything he can to rescue me.

* * *

WHEN I WAKE THIS MORNING, something seems different. I can't place it, almost as if the wind has changed. The door opens and Miss. Hughes enters with a tray with more food than usual.

She sets it down and sneers, "Today you will prepare for your wedding."

"Today?" My heart jumps a million miles, and she nods. "Despite your laziness, the reverend has vowed to continue your bible studies personally. You will marry now his mourning period has ended and tomorrow you will wake up as his wife."

Just the mere thought of that makes me feel nauseous, and she snaps, "You don't deserve a fine man like him. He is a saint for taking you on."

I ignore her words and say in a rush, "My baby. Will I see her today?"

The expression on her face is not a pleasant one as she says with apparent glee, "Your baby has been relocated."

My eyes widen as she sneers, "Permanently. You will never see her again."

From somewhere deep inside comes a rage I never knew was there. My fists curl and my blood boils as I well and truly lose my cool.

Grabbing the pitcher of water, I throw it hard at the disgusting woman and, as she recoils, I rush at her like a bear defending its cub.

She puts up her hands to ward me off, but I am too far gone for that. I deliver an uppercut punch that would floor any professional boxer and she screams as I knock her to the ground. I don't stop there, and rain blows to her face as I unleash the beast inside me, my grief overpowering my sense and only when a rope is fastened around my neck and tightened cruelly, do I gasp for air as the reverend pulls me to the ground, delivering a well-aimed kick in my side for good measure.

"ENOUGH!" he yells and as I try to loosen the rope around my throat, he says in an icy voice, "How dare you attack Miss. Hughes. You are a vixen; a wild uncontrollable savage and I will not allow that kind of behavior in my home."

I stare up in fright as his boot connects with my body, and I experience a blinding pain and then he reaches down and wraps his hands around my neck and squeezes until my eyes blur and my lungs burn.

It would be so easy to give into it and just as I begin to lose consciousness, he releases me and I drag in huge gulps of air as he hisses, "You will marry me today in front of the entire town because if you make one false move, your baby will suffer."

"My baby…" The tears fall as I sob. "She told me my baby was gone."

"So, you're a liar as well as a whore."

I blink up at him as he helps Miss. Hughes to her feet. Then he says calmly, "Miss. Hughes. Did you tell this whore her baby had gone?"

"No, sir. Of course not. I would never lie. It's a sin."

"But you said…"

I stare at her in disbelief and am rewarded by a sharp slap around the face courtesy of the reverend.

"How dare you cast aspersions on a fine woman's character. Your punishment will be severe."

He grabs the rope and drags me across the room and sits on the wooden chair, hauling me over his lap while the sullen housekeeper watches. Then he pulls my dress around my waist and delivers painful blows on my ass in front of the woman who tricked me.

"How many, Miss. Hughes."

The reverend says calmly, and she says in a voice devoid of all emotion. "Twenty."

As the blows rain down on me, hard and unyielding, I will not give her the satisfaction of seeing me cry.

I am made to count every single one and after the final one, he pushes me to the ground and says to the housekeeper.

"After our wedding, stand by with the scissors. We will cut her hair and then shave her head. She will be forced to be a devoted wife and renounce evil."

Miss. Hughes nods and says cruelly, "It will be my pleasure to assist you, sir."

The reverend stands and casts a cruel look in my direction and says smoothly. "Prepare her for the service. You have one hour."

The only thing keeping me going is that I will leave this place today. In front of the entire town, I will refuse to marry this bastard and reveal the bruises he has inflicted on me. I will fall on their mercy and ask for their help because there is no way in hell I am ever setting foot inside this house again.

CHAPTER 16

JONNY

I've watched every move the reverend makes and noted his routine. I have monitored Miss. Hughes and memorized every inch of their day.

To my knowledge, nobody knows I'm still here except for Arthur and so I'm surprised to receive an unexpected visit from an unlikely visitor just before sunrise.

A gentle knock on the door has me reaching for my gun and yet when I open it, I'm amazed to see Arthur with a nervous looking passenger in his wagon.

"Purity?" I ask and he nods, looking worried.

"I'm sorry, Jonny, she said she needed to speak with you. She discovered I was hiding you out here and demanded to come."

"Did she now?" It makes me smile because despite appearing as if she would bend in a stiff breeze, Purity, as it turns out, has balls of steel.

"Bring her in." I say quickly, dragging on a t-shirt out of respect for the lady. I have no problem with the cabin because my military training has taught me to keep things in an orderly fashion and so when they enter, they sit at the table that is free from anything at all.

"Coffee?" I ask, and they both nod.

"Thanks."

I can tell Purity is nervous and is finding it difficult to look at me and so I say gently, "You wanted to tell me something."

She nods, her eyes wide and afraid. "Please, nobody can discover I'm here."

"Of course, but you took a chance coming at all." I say kindly. "How did you know I was still in town?"

She peers at Arthur and whispers, "I followed Mr. Gaston. I saw him load supplies into his truck and take the road up to the mountain. I waited and saw him return in less than an hour and I knew he had a cabin up here. I figured someone was staying in it and guessed it was you."

She looks so proud of her detective work it makes me like her even more and I share an amused grin with Arthur, who holds his hands up.

"She got me. She slipped me a note telling me she discovered what I was doing and told me to bring her here before her parents woke up. We don't have long."

"So, tell me what you need me to hear, darlin'." I smile and she blushes a little and whispers as if she can be overheard. "The wedding is today."

Arthur glances at me with a worried frown and I say quickly, "I thought it was in two days' time."

"I heard my father talking to my mother. He told her the reverend has decided to bring it forward because he has important work to do, and it can't wait any longer."

"And you're sure it's today?"

She nods. "Yes."

She bites her bottom lip and whispers, "Please, Jonny. You must stop it."

I consider my words carefully and say, "My daughter."

Her eyes widen and I fix her with a hard stare. "Do you know where she is?"

I'm not even surprised when she nods, "With Miss. Hughes' sister in Brindley Ridge."

I am mad at myself for not thinking about Purity earlier. She appears to make it her business to know about everything, and her eyes widen as she says, "I have a plan."

This time I do laugh and Arthur stares with amusement as she snaps, "Don't underestimate me, Jonny Santos. I'm tougher than you think. The reason I haven't told you is because Faith swore me to secrecy. How was I to know she told you about Hope?"

I must admire her loyalty and say quickly, "What's your plan?"

She takes a deep breath.

"Mr. Gaston will take me to Miss. Hughes' house, and we will tell her that the Reverend wants the baby back. She must be at the wedding and if she refuses, we will go to the cops and report her for kidnapping."

"That's your plan. But what about your parents? They will learn you are missing when they head to the wedding?"

"That is where the second part of my plan comes in. You rescue Faith from the Church and come and meet us in Brindley Ridge. Mr. Gaston will return home and I will head to Chicago."

"Why Chicago?" I'm amazed she even knows of its existence, and she says with determination. "I have business there."

"Business?"

Arthur appears as amazed as I am, and she nods with a resolve that tells me I did indeed underestimate Purity Sanders.

"*My* business, Jonny. I only need the means to get there."

She says quickly as we hesitate. "We don't have long. We must leave now before I'm reported missing. Mr. Gaston needs to be at the service, or they will know he had a hand in this."

"And you can deal with Rosemary alone?"

I'm doubtful and Purity grins. "I can deal with her. I'm not just a pretty face, Jonny. There's not a lot to do in Heaven but pray and sharpen your skills and Jed Turner has been teaching me to fight since I was six years old."

"Well, I'll be." Arthur bursts out laughing. "Jed Turner is much like you were, Jonny. That doesn't surprise me in the least."

Once again, I stare at the pretty blonde with doe eyes and porcelain skin in a new light. Who am I to deny her freedom, especially when she is risking everything to help her closest friend?

So, I nod. "It's a good plan. Don't fuck it up. Wait until we get there before approaching Rosemary. Keep her under observation, but I repeat, do not deal with this yourself. There is too much riding on it."

She nods, but I see a little of the light dim in her eyes.

As they make to leave, she turns and, to my surprise, throws her arms around me and hugs me tightly, whispering, "Look after Faith, Jonny. She loves you and what she did was a result of that."

She pulls away and grins. "Now go and get your girl, soldier."

Arthur grins as I catch his eye because words are failing me right now. Who is this girl and where did she come from because it's obvious Purity doesn't belong in Heaven? I'm curious what is waiting for her in Chicago that has fired her up to do the unthinkable because if she is discovered, her life will never be the same again.

As I watch them leave, I waste no time and dash out a quick text.

It's happening today. 10 am. I have confirmation Hope is at Rosemary Hughes. If you get there before me, watch out for an angel that goes by the name of Purity. Approach with caution.

It amuses me as I press send and as I set about my preparations, it's with a great sense of excitement because it's time to go and do what I do best and, as Purity said, go and get my girls.

CHAPTER 17

FAITH

I am physically shaking. I can't believe this is happening. Miss. Hughes was not gentle with me when she tied my hair into a tight bun, and I mean really tight. So tight it causes my eyes to water, and it's as if I'm gripped in steel jaws, not bobby pins.

There is no make-up except foundation to cover the bruises. Not that they do a good job and so she shakes her head and snaps, "You must keep your veil on to prevent the congregation staring at the result of your sin."

My sin? She has got to be kidding me because the biggest sinners in this town are these two.

The dress she has made me wear is plain, practical and scratches like hell. A simple white dress that I'm certain is about to be present at wedding number five. Knowing the previous occupants died because of this dress, makes me want to be physically sick. There is something sinister about life in the reverend's home and I pray I'm not about to discover what that is first hand.

I know he has been held back by the period of mourning and I'm guessing married life will be no bed of roses. Just imagining what that will involve freezes my blood. The fact I'll be controlled by the two monsters inside this house tells me why the previous occupants took the easy way out.

If it wasn't for Hope, I would be considering that option right now, but I've never been one to give into a challenge and I would rather fight my way out than die.

Self-preservation is high on my to do list right now and if there is a God, I will not be returning here with a metal band on my finger. Today or any day in the future.

Reverend Peters has already left by the time we are ready, which I'm grateful for. As I follow Miss. Hughes outside, I'm astonished to see my father waiting with his car door open.

The veil covers my face, and I search for any hint of concern at all in his expression, but there is nothing but grave acceptance for my situation.

As we step forward, Miss. Hughes says politely, "Good morning, Sir."

He nods. "Good morning, Miss. Hughes."

Without a glance in my direction, he points to the back seat and as I slide inside, my heart is cold. Where is the love? Where is the duty of care he should feel in bucket loads for his daughter? It's obvious he has washed his hands of me and couldn't give a shit about my situation.

Then there's Hope. He can't even bring himself to mention her name, or even look at her. He has always pretended she doesn't exist, which hurt deeper than I wanted it to.

I have always craved his affection but never receive any. I'm not surprised that he sold me out because he apparently couldn't wait to be rid of me. I'm an embarrassment. That's always been obvious. Now he can enjoy an elevated status in the town as the father-in-law of the most powerful man in Heaven. My husband.

I shiver as the possibility of that strikes me cold.

Not fucking likely. Not if I have anything to do with it and as the car starts its fateful journey, I prepare myself for the fight of my life.

Our journey is spent in silence, largely because Miss. Hughes sits beside me like a demon on my shoulder. However, as soon as the car reaches its destination, she heads inside with a parting sneer.

As we wait outside, the warm sun is a welcome addition to the wedding party and I love the heat it brings to my frozen body, calming me and reassuring me that everything will be okay. I listen to the birds singing in the nearby tree. The sound is like nature's serenade, pure and sweet. Completely out of place at this wedding.

My father stands silently waiting for the music to start, signifying my descent into madness, so I take my chance and, lifting the veil, stare at him for any sign of compassion at all.

"Pa, please." I feel the tears glisten in my eyes as I face him with brutality written all over my face. "Please don't do this. The man is deranged. He is sick, I'm telling you. I'm afraid for my life. For Hope's life. He has taken her."

I get nothing back but a look of derision and, in desperation, I clutch at his hand, causing him to pull back as if I've stabbed him as I plead, "I'm begging you. Take me home. Take me anywhere but here. I can't marry that monster. You will be attending my funeral next if you go through with this."

He leans forward and hisses, "The reverend told us it wouldn't be pretty. That banishing evil comes at a price."

I step back. "You knew he was going to do this?"

To be honest, I'm surprised that I'm even shocked about that.

"Of course. You are a sinner, Faith. You went against everything we have ever taught you and willingly committed a sin when you allowed the devil to plant his seed in your womb. You bore a bastard child and you will pay penance for that."

"But I'm your daughter. You should love and protect me. How could you?"

"Because you let me down when you sinned against me."

"Against you! What are you talking about?"

I can't believe what I'm hearing, and he snaps, "Do you know what happened when you ran, Faith? Do you know what it was like to walk down the street under the glare of disapproval? We were pitied, Faith. The town was disgusted with our family because we raised a disobedient child who was given too much freedom. They blamed us. Your mother and me. We weren't good enough parents. We had failed in our duty. We were shunned and dis-invited to everything. Made to sit at the back of the church and singled out for blame. The reverend made sure we were the subject of all his teachings about evil and allowing it into Heaven. We were pariah's, Faith and all because of you."

"Is that why you brought me back?"

I can still remember waking up after having Hope with my parents by my bed, demanding I return home with them. I resisted but mom promised she would help care for us and as a new mother with no means of caring for my child, I had no choice.

He hisses. "It was our path to salvation. The reverend told us we must pay the lord back by sacrificing the bastard child, along with its mother. He would tear the devil from inside you both and, in doing so, would grant us redemption."

"You're sick. The whole fucking town is sick!"

I scream as my father raises his hand, the sting of his knuckles cracking against my face drowned out by the opening bars of the wedding march.

He wastes no time in pulling down my veil and growling,

"Now do your duty and pay us back for ruining our lives. You have no choice, Faith. This is your punishment for your sins, and you can burn in hell for all I care. You and that bastard child you brought into the world."

The tears blind me as I stumble after him, his grip on my wrist a painful reminder that I have nowhere to run to. There is only one person left who can save me and I pray to God, he doesn't leave it too late.

The church is crowded. There isn't a spare seat inside and as we enter, the townsfolk stand and stare ahead with rigid backs. They don't even look at us as my father drags me down the aisle, crying helplessly and begging for help.

My voice is pitiful and edged with pain as I struggle against the powerful grip of the man who just spoke his way out of my life forever. I had a father once who, as it turns out, wasn't man enough for the job and so I kick and scream as he marches me down the aisle, the music getting louder to drown out my protest.

Two men step forward when we reach the altar and I recognize one is Purity's father and the other one is Amos Budleigh, the town doctor.

They grip hold of my arms on either side and hold me up as I stare at the man who is the biggest bastard in town.

My husband if he gets his way, and he stares down from the pulpit with anger flashing in his eyes as I sob and scream like a wailing angel.

"SILENCE!" he yells, and I swear you could hear a feather drop as he sneers, "The whole town will witness the hard work I have ahead of me."

He points to me and almost screams. "The devil is among us! It has consumed this poor pathetic creature, and that is what happens when you let evil inside your mind."

The congregation murmur and I don't expect I'm helping

my claim to sanity as I yell, "Don't let him do this. The man's a deranged monster. He's sick in the head and you must stand up to him."

Their disapproval hits me along with their disgust as my pleas fall on deaf ears and Reverend Peters yells, "You can see the Devil at work, right before your eyes. Stay strong and pray to God to deliver us from this evil. She will become my wife and I will do my best to cure her within the protective sanctity of marriage. Praise be to God for his wisdom and help with saving her poor soul."

It's a good job the men are holding me up because my knees have weakened, and my sobs are all I can hear over his vile words. This is a disaster. There is nobody here to help me and as the reverend starts reciting the marriage vows, I really believe this is the end for me.

CHAPTER 18

JONNY

I am like a feral beast straining on the leash, and it takes every inch of self-control I possess not to rush in and ruin a carefully thought-out plan.

"Easy, soldier."

A rough hand sits on my shoulder and if I am grateful for anything, it's my brothers who arrived in Heaven earlier this morning.

They flew out, bikes and all, in the early hours and made their way to the cabin.

Now we are staked out around the church, Arthur's warning noted loud and clear. We can't take any chances if the townsfolk are carrying and only a fool would march into a hostile environment with no backup.

However, when I saw Mr. Monroe strike his own daughter, I was half on my feet before Ryder ordered me to remain calm.

"Easy for you to say." I growl, hating that he's right and he whispers, "You'll get your revenge on him, but it must be the right time."

I know he's right, as always, and as I catch the expression

on the man to my right's face, I'm comforted knowing they hate this shit just as much as I do. Snake has always been Ryder's second in command. In the military and when he formed The Twisted Reapers MC. The cobra tattoo he wears on his arm is a sign of bravery every one of the Reapers share and as we lie in wait for battle, I am comforted knowing I have their support.

Most of the team are here with me, as well as a group sent to Brindley Ridge to secure my daughter. The remaining soldiers stay at the compound, protecting our home and all who live there. Like this town, we are a curious community living a life that many don't understand. Shrouded in secrecy and operating outside the law. The perfect people to bring down a tyrant and our work never hits the news. We are untraceable, unpunishable, and operating with the blessing of our fine government. No, Reverend Peters is about to discover just what happens when you go against the constitution, because he will not escape this time.

The music begins and I watch with growing anger as Faith is dragged kicking and screaming into the white wooden church.

As soon as the doors close, Ryder holds up his hand and starts the countdown.

I hear her cries above the music, and I swear every nerve I possess is screaming at me right now.

It's an interminable wait before he brings down his hand and one by one, in a pre-arranged order, we move on command, circling the church like a deadly virus, ready to deliver the inhabitants of this small town into an early grave. If they fight back, that is.

The plan is to cut out the cancer destroying it and then let the authorities move in to clean up after him. They will drag this town into the modern world, whether they like it or not. Cops, rules, and technology will move in and restore order to a place that doesn't even know what that is. Counselors to un-indoctrinate the inhabitants and courts to punish the guilty.

But first we have our fun.

Once the Reapers have surrounded the church, the rest stand behind me, waiting for the show to begin.

Snake whispers at my shoulder, "I've always wanted to storm a wedding and rescue a bride. This is a tick off my bucket list."

Ryder rolls his eyes as I growl, "Glad to be of service."

We listen to Reverend Peters yelling his usual shit, and then as he starts reciting the wedding service, Ryder says roughly, "The stage is yours, soldier. Have fun with this."

I waste no time and with one swift kick of my boot, the door crashes open and a sea of shocked faces turn to stare at me, as I stride into that church and say loudly, "Take your fucking hands off her."

The wave of disapproval hits me as I stare with rage at the men holding Faith, who turn and as their hands drop, she rips the veil from her head and starts running.

"STOP!" The reverend screams but as she falls into my arms, there is no man present who would dare stand up against me as, one by one, I am surrounded by a wall of muscle, ink, and menace as my brothers file in behind me.

When I see the bruises on Faith's face, it physically hurts and bending down, I whisper, "He will pay for what he's done to you."

Her eyes fill with tears, and she whispers, "But what about Hope?"

"She's fine. The rest of my club is guarding her."

She collapses with relief against my chest as Reverend Peters starts clapping loudly, causing us all to turn and stare.

"Well, if it isn't hell paying us a visit. You know what to do, men."

I catch Arthur's face as he stares at me with resignation as the men of the town reach for their guns at the same time as the Reapers pull machine guns out from behind their backs.

I quickly pull Faith behind me, and she is instantly shielded by a wall of Reapers, and I aim my own gun straight at the reverend's head and snarl, "Do you want a shoot-out in your church, reverend because guess what, our weapons are bigger than yours."

As I speak, Snake tosses a grenade down the aisle, more to prove a point than anything, and I yell, "Run!"

It's almost amusing to watch the mad panic that follows as the people of Heaven run for their lives. We step to one side as they stampede to the door and completely ignore the reverend who screams at them to stop. Snake takes Faith, accompanied by Flash, and I am assured of her safety as I face the reverend with Ryder by my side.

The grenade stares up at us with impudence because nobody knew it would never go off. A dummy run before the main event but it had the desired result, leaving the two of us and Reverend Peters, who suddenly doesn't look so confident anymore.

As I move toward him, he starts praying. Uttering jumbled words as he clutches his hands together and prays to the cross on the wall.

Words like, 'deliver me from evil' and 'spare my soul' hit me and then, as I almost reach him, he draws a gun from inside his jacket and fires.

The bullet bounces close to my ear and then one shot brings him down screaming, as the bullet rips through the hand clinging onto his gun. It falls as he stumbles, and I kick it away, grabbing him by the neck and slamming his face against the pulpit.

Ryder lowers his gun and shakes his head.

"Fucking bad move, reverend. Fucking bad move."

He reaches my side and casts his hard, disapproving stare at the man shivering in my arms and says in his deadly voice, "Just so you know, you are no man of God. If the devil controls anyone around here, I'm looking at him."

He fixes him with a withering glare and says in a voice laced with vengeance, "Finish the job, soldier, and make it count."

As his heavy wooden boots tread the path out of here, Reverend Peters screams, "You won't get away with this! The Lord will strike you down. You are sinners and you will pay with your soul."

Ryder merely laughs and says over his shoulder, "I'll take my chances in the afterlife, reverend. Save a place for me in hell."

As the door slams behind him, for the first time in my life Reverend Peters looks at me with fear in his eyes as I growl, "From one sinner to another, it's time to pay for your sins and guess what, I'm going to make sure it's brutal."

CHAPTER 19

FAITH

*R*elief, love, fear, and hatred are all battling for control as I am escorted from the church with a real fear for the man I've left inside. Not the reverend, definitely not him, but when a shot rings out, I scream and try to head back in.

The scary man holding me says firmly, "Not happening, darlin'. You're going to trust that man of yours and wait for him to do his job."

"But?" The tears run down my face as the other man says kindly, "He'll be fine. Sinner is a bad-assed motherfucker who is like a cockroach. He'll always survive."

"Watch your filthy mouth soldier, there's a lady present." The other guy growls and I'm shocked when the other guy says gently, "I'm sorry, darlin', I apologize."

It's as if I'm in another world as I stare in disbelief at the sight before me. The town is surrounded by men who scare the shit out of me, all wearing the exact same leather jacket that Jonny was wearing.

"Don't be afraid, darlin'." A husky whisper in my ear

comforts me. "We look like shit, but we only have your best interests at heart. Nobody will be hurt unless they deserve it."

I catch sight of my mom and dad, and the expressions on their faces confuse me. Dad is angry. It's obvious as he stares at me as if he wants to shoot me dead himself. But it's mom's expression that builds my tears. She is half smiling and looks so relieved it surprises me. She stares at me with a small smile and, if anything, appears happy for me. I'm so confused and as I glance around, I notice that one person is missing.

I can't find my best friend anywhere. I see her parents staring at me as if I murdered her somehow, and I wonder what's happened.

However, there is no time to think about it because suddenly, the bikers start moving among the crowd, grabbing the townsfolk's weapons, and piling them in a heap on the ground. One by one, they search the people of Heaven and disarm them of their weapons. Shouting at them to lie on the dusty ground with their hands above their heads.

I watch my own parents shoved to the ground and if I'm not mistaken, the heavy boot that connects with my father's body was a deliberate move, causing the men beside me to chuckle softly. "Good one, Maverick." They shout out to a scary-looking guy with the jaded eyes of a man who's seen it all before.

The scary guy with the snake tattoo growls, "Man, I wish I had five minutes alone with that bastard."

The other guy nods. "Fucking disgrace treating his daughter like that."

I can't take it all in and stare open-mouthed as the people I grew up with, lie on the ground at the mercy of the bikers and then I turn as the door to the church opens, and a guy that immediately questions everything I've ever done in life steps out with a rough, "Is the area secure?"

"Yes, sir." They all shout, and he crosses over to me and says with a gentle twinkle in his eye.

"Then we wait."

"Jonny?" I say in a hoarse whisper, and he shares a glance with the men and grins.

"Let him have his fun first, then we'll head over to pick up your baby."

"Really." I can't quite believe this is happening, and he says gently, "I have a daughter too and there is nothing I wouldn't do to keep her safe. We are here to be the family you deserve, darlin' and you have nothing to fear from us. Either of you. Mind you..."

He grins at the men beside him. "We can't help you with your other problem."

"What problem?" I'm confused, and he jerks his thumb in the direction of the church.

"Sinner. You have my sympathy because it's doubtful that bastard is going to let you out of his sight now you're in it."

The other men laugh and yet I'm happy at his words. The trouble is, I doubt Jonny will want me after this because of what I did to him. It will take a lot of forgiveness and I'm not sure if we will make it, but right now, in this moment, he is everything I want in life, him and my baby.

My family.

CHAPTER 20

JONNY

*R*everend Peters is fucking terrified. His eyes are wide and his skin pale. His breathing is labored and not just because I am holding him in an iron grip.

A sense of calm washes over me as I hold his life in my hands and then with a wicked idea, I pull him to his own altar and growl, "Kneel, you bastard."

I almost want him to refuse, but he cowers down before me as I hold my gun to his head and press in hard, causing him to physically shake.

I say in a loud voice, "Gloria Jones. Died by drowning. Sandy Richards fell out of the top window of your house and broke her neck. Gayle Matthews shot herself, and Agatha Little hung herself in the woods behind your home."

I shake my head and regard him with a ferocious expression. "That's quite a list and pretty careless, wouldn't you agree, Reverend?"

He sniffs as I press the steel in deeper.

"I have been informed their deaths weren't the accidents you pretended they were."

"You know nothing." He hisses and I laugh out loud.

"There is a witness who has told us everything."

"What witness?" For the first time, I watch the reverend's walls crumble.

"Miss. Hughes." I say, taking a chance and he stills and says quickly, "I don't believe you. She would never talk about me. She idolizes me."

"I didn't say which Miss. Hughes now, did I?"

He stiffens as the realization causes him to wake up to judgment day and I carry on.

"It turns out sisters talk, and she had quite a story to tell when my brothers paid her a visit this morning."

He says nothing and I growl, "As I said before, pretty careless, wouldn't you say? I mean, if you're going to cause another person's death, at least be truthful about it."

I crouch down and press the gun against his temple and whisper, "Guess what? You're going to die today."

His eyes are wide, and I glance down as the sound of liquid hits the floor, telling me he's pissed himself through fright, which is just the reaction I wanted.

I glance at the window and, checking its open, I say loudly, "So, tell me, Reverend. What did Gloria Jones do to deserve death?"

He yells, "She was a sinner! All women are the spawn of Eve, put on earth to tempt God-fearing men. You should know, you were tempted by one of them. A whore."

He cries out as I strike him hard around the face. Much like he did to Faith and his pitiful wail causes me to snarl, "So you can beat a woman, but you can't take it from a man."

He spits out blood on the floor and yells, "They were all the same. The devil's work. Gloria, Sandy, Gayle, and Agatha. Four sirens whose sole purpose in life was to tempt me. To break me. They were God's test, and I did what he told me to do. I resisted them. I punished them. I cleansed them!"

He is almost screaming now, which suits me just fine, and

I push him further. "You killed them, didn't you, Reverend? You made it look like an accident and you sent them to an early grave."

"I *delivered* them!" He hollers. "I did what God told me to do. I beat the sin out of them and tried to cleanse their minds by filling it with the good, pure words of the bible. They taunted me with their large eyes and impudent bodies." He hisses. "They tried to drag me down and make me fall, but I was too strong for them. I punished them for their sins and used them as the whores they were."

"You raped them." I growl and he laughs out loud like the maniac he is.

"You call it rape. I call it teaching them a lesson. They would experience the dominance of men. Put them in their place so they could understand their bodies were good for only one thing. Bearing a child. I stripped them of their looks, dignity and humanity to teach THEM A LESSON!"

He is screaming as his twisted features stare up at me, revealing the crazy inside his mind. My gun is pressing into his head, and he's almost forgotten it's there as he laughs like a madman.

"It's what I do. I keep Heaven in the light of God. I punish sinners, which you know only too well."

"Ah, yes." I sense the anger building inside me as he refers to my own cleansing at his hands and I say roughly, "You took a young boy and you beat him. You stripped him of his dignity, and you kept him locked in a cage. You taunted him, you goaded him, and you terrified him."

I take a deep breath, trying to remain in control of my shit, and say in a deadly voice, "You whipped him, caned him, and throttled him. You beat him to within an inch of his life and then you made him beg for forgiveness. That child was six years old. That child was me."

He merely sneers and spits on my boot. "You were my biggest failure. You were your parent's biggest failure and this town's biggest failure. You deserved everything you got and I'm only sorry I didn't bury you along with the other sinners I tried to help."

As I stare at the maniac at my feet, a sense of calm fills me.

I think about the child I was, sitting on my shoulder now, watching his aggressor get what's coming to him. I am surrounded by the ghosts of the women he murdered, and I stand with Faith and Hope on either side of me as I prepare to do what is inevitable.

Most of all, I have the backing of my brothers because without them, I would not be as strong, so I grab the reverend's gun that's resting nearby and force it into his hand and cover it with mine.

For a second, he grins, thinking he has regained the upper hand, and I whisper, "You are not worth my time. Just for your information, Heaven is about to be dragged into the modern world and everyone will learn how evil you are. You will be spoken about as the demon who took over this town disguised as a man of God. They will think of you as the devil because that is who really controls your evil mind and so, maybe now is the perfect time to send you back to him."

His wide eyes fill with rage with every word I speak and as he makes to argue I take his hand and force his own gun into his mouth and as I use his finger to pull the trigger, the last words he hears are, "Rot in hell you bastard."

As his head explodes in my hand, I feel a sense of relief that it's over. As his blood rains down, it signifies a cleansing of sorts. My past has been blown away with his spirit and he will never be able to harm anyone again.

I could have beaten him. I could have tortured him, and I could have made it brutal. However, I'm not him and I never will be and that was a fitting end for a bastard who had the soul of the devil disguised as one of God's chosen.

One thing I'm certain of, Heaven is no longer an option for Reverend Peters, and the world will be a much better place without him in it.

CHAPTER 21

FAITH

There is an eerie silence as the reverend's voice spills from the church outside. I swear the entire town turns toward the open window and listens to the confessions of a madman. With every word he speaks, a part of my soul falls away because I never knew. I doubt anyone did what lengths he went to and for so many years.

We trusted him. We feared him, which, as it turns out, was for a very good reason.

He was a serial killer masquerading as a priest. He was the man the town looked to for guidance. To speak about their innermost thoughts and beg for forgiveness. We have crowded into his church every day for the past thirty years and lived our lives through his teachings because we hoped he was setting us on the right path.

He has made a mockery of everything we believed in, and his confession reminds us what fools we were. What fools we are, because every single person in this town lapped up everything he preached and never questioned him at all.

My heart reaches out to his many victims, and I shiver

when I remember what it was like under his rule. My life was about to become unbearable and now, what now? I still don't have the answer to that.

I swear nobody spoke at all as his words rang out loud and damning his soul to hell.

I glance at my father, who is lying on the floor, his hands above his head, still and frozen in place as the words of the man he trusted washes over him like acid rain.

It must burn knowing you have been made a fool of. Every person here who believed in him must be feeling like the biggest idiot alive right now.

Then there are the ferocious men who brought light on the subject. Standing over their captives with a fearsome silence and expressions of disgust for what this town has done.

We are no better than Reverend Peters. We allowed it to happen and when a shot rings out it shatters the silence and I scream as I make to run toward the church.

"Jonny!" I yell as I am held back by my two protectors and the man who commands them says with a slight shake of his head, "I wouldn't go in there if I were you."

"Jonny!" I sob as I struggle in their arms and then my heart almost stops beating as the door opens and the man himself walks out, covered in blood but with a smile on his face.

I am finally released and as I fall into his bloodied arms, I couldn't care less. As they wrap around my shivering body, I cry so hard with relief that he made it.

He rests his hand on the back of my head and leans down, whispering, "It's over, baby. You're free. We're all free."

"You mean..." I stare up at him with hope and he grins, revealing the man I fell in love in with. "Dead, baby. Let's just say he repented of his sins and took the easy way out."

The biker beside him chuckles at that and says in a husky drawl, "If you say so, soldier."

As the townsfolk start murmuring, we hear sirens wailing in the distance, and I stare at Jonny in fright.

"You should go. The cops are here. They'll arrest you."

I'm frantic as I imagine Jonny and his club being arrested for murder, but all I get is a low laugh, followed by another one from behind me.

"Don't worry about us, baby, we're the good guys, remember?" He drops me a wink and, as the first car reaches us, I sense a tidal wave of relief from the bodies on the ground.

More cops than I have ever seen descend into the chaotic aftermath and to everyone's surprise, the sheriff slaps the man with Jonny on the back and says in a friendly manner, "It's good to see you, sir."

"Sheriff." He replies with a low husky drawl, and I watch in amazement as they head off, deep in conversation and as the bikers begin to disperse, Jonny says quickly, "We don't have time to watch what happens next. We have a baby to bring home."

"Hope!"

My heart lurches as he smiles. "Aptly named, darlin'."

Mr. Gaston runs toward us and says in an urgent whisper, "Come on. I'll take you there."

We waste no time, and I don't even glance back to check on my parents and yet before we make it to the car, I hear a loud, "JONNY!"

It comes at us like machine gun fire, stopping Jonny in his tracks and he slowly turns to face his father, who, by the look of him, is not too happy.

"What?" Jonny snaps and his father says angrily, "What have you done?"

Jonny sighs as his father steps closer and hisses. "You are a cold-hearted killer, and you will be punished for your crimes."

Jonny says nothing and just shrugs, which makes his father incensed.

"You may think you have it all figured out, but you are deluded." His father says in a bitter voice. "We always knew you were the spawn of the devil. Boisterous, rough and disobedient from almost the day you could walk. You were a fighter, callous and unruly, and it's no wonder we sent you to the reverend to be cleansed."

Jonny breaks away and gets in his father's face and hisses, "I was a child!" he yells. "I was fucking six years old when you sent me to that monster. You were never my dad. You were never there for me. All my life I've felt as if I was an inconvenience. An irritant to tolerate and a punching bag for your anger. You never loved me. You never listened to me, and you certainly never wanted me. Arthur was more like a father to me than you ever were, so congratulations, I hereby relieve you of your burden of responsibility. You disowned me when I returned from fighting for our country. Fighting to keep Americans safe and protect our constitution. You called me a brutal sinner and told me to never come back here at all. Well, now you've got your wish, because this is the last you will ever see of me."

He pushes his father hard, who makes the error of trying to strike his son and I stare as my jaw drops to the floor as with one loud roar and an almighty punch, Jonny strikes his father to the ground.

Then he turns and the wild gleam in his eye should terrify me. It should make me question every reason why I love this man, but all it does is confirm the most important thing. He is *my* man, and we belong together because I understand exactly how he is feeling now, because I feel the same. I know what he went through because I went through the same and so, I reach out my hand and smile.

"Let's go."

He nods and as his large hand closes over mine, we step into Mr. Gaston's car and don't look back.

CHAPTER 22

JONNY

I try not to dwell on the past. I try to live in the moment, but when we leave Heaven behind, it's as if my life flashes before my eyes.

We sit in silence because words are meaningless now. There is too much to process, and as Faith's hand rests in mine, I have an overwhelming desire to be closer. It's always been a physical ache where she is concerned and so I wrap my arm around her trembling shoulders and love how her head rests on my shoulder.

She doesn't even care that my jacket has been decorated with another man's brains. This tells me she's strong. But will she be strong enough for what happens next?

In all the time I've lived among the Reapers, I've never questioned the life we live. At first it shocked me, but I soon grew accustomed to our way of life. Reverend Peters would liken it to Sodom and Gomorrah. To me, it's more like Heaven than Hell. It's my home and there is nothing at all that I don't love about living at the Rubicon, but Faith is a different story entirely. She has never lived anywhere but Heaven and I'm not sure how she will cope with Hell.

After a while, Arthur says gruffly, "I want to thank you, Jonny."

"You don't owe me anything, even thanks." I growl and he shakes his head as he turns right at the junction, the sign to Brindley Ridge indicating the way.

"You saved the people in Heaven, and they didn't even realize they needed saving."

"But you did."

I state a fact, and he sighs heavily. "I concluded a long time ago it wasn't right. I heard stories, the whispered conversations about things that made my heart break. Don't blame the people, they knew nothing else but I'm glad you came home, Jonny. I'm happy I helped you and I wish you every happiness in your future. Just don't be a stranger."

When we turned away from the town I grew up in, I made a vow to never return. It makes me laugh that within the hour, I am already breaking that vow. I would do anything for Arthur and Martha, so I say gruffly, "You should come and visit me sometime."

Arthur laughs out loud. "Neither I or my wife are ready for that kind of wake-up call."

Faith is quietly listening, but her eyes are wide, reminding me once again we have many battles ahead.

I bear the weight of responsibility heavy on my shoulders and turn to her, and I hope my smile is one of reassurance. "You will love it, Faith. There is nothing to fear where we're heading."

"Where are we, heading, I mean?" She whispers, her voice strangely afraid.

"Home, baby. To be a family and be safe."

She says nothing at all and just smiles at me tentatively and I experience a surge of protective love for the timid woman who claimed my heart.

As the small town comes into view, I am more nervous

than I've ever been in my life as I contemplate what is waiting for us.

We turn down a street just off the main one and I immediately note where our destination is, due to the number of bikes parked outside.

As we pull up, I see a pretty white wooden house with a small veranda on which sits the most terrifying sight.

Arthur whistles, "Good lord, Miss. Hughes must be shitting a brick."

It makes us laugh, but I can see why he's concerned. Five heavily tattooed beasts are sitting on her swing and leaning against the balustrade as they enjoy the sunshine, and from the number of bikes outside, I'm guessing more are inside.

As we exit the car, Faith's grip tightens on my hand and I whisper, "Don't be afraid of the Reapers, baby. Be more afraid of life without them."

She says nothing and pulls me with urgency toward the small house, and I understand she is anxious to be reunited with her daughter. *Our* daughter and my heart beats fast as I prepare to meet Hope for the very first time.

"Hey, Sinner. Congratulations, brother."

Jet steps forward and shakes my hand.

Tyson does the same, followed by Brewer, who says with rare emotion. "Welcome to fatherhood, Jonny."

For a moment, I experience a sense of pride I wasn't expecting. I'm a father now and, unlike my own, I'm determined to be the right kind of father. The one I always wanted and so I take Faith's hand and squeeze it hard and whisper, "Let's go and get our girl."

We step inside the small house and the first thing I see is Miss. Hughes looking utterly terrified as she sobs on the couch, flanked on either side by two bikers who are offering her no sympathy.

Then Faith cries out when she sees Purity holding a small bundle wrapped in a cotton blanket and my heart shifts when I see my daughter for the first time.

Purity steps forward, the tears running down her face as she holds Hope out to Faith, who takes her carefully into her arms. I swallow the lump in my throat as she leans down and kisses her and the tears spill onto her as Faith whispers, "Mommy's here, honey. It's all over now. Nothing will ever separate us again."

It's such a moving scene you could hear a feather take flight and then she looks up at Purity and whispers, "Thank you so much."

Purity is crying too and Tyson growls, "Fuck. I never could stand watching a woman cry. I'll wait outside."

At the sound of his voice, Faith turns and the joy on her face makes me smile as she heads my way and whispers, "This is your daughter, Jonny. Say hello."

I gaze down at the prettiest little face I have ever seen. So angelic, so perfect, and so incredible that she came from the two of us.

Her wide baby blue eyes are staring at me, and an unconditional bolt of love hits me square in the heart. I have actual tears in my eyes as I stare at my daughter for the very first time and then open my arms as Faith whispers, "Hold her."

As the small bundle settles in my arms, raw emotion grips my heart as I lift her up and drop a light kiss on her sweet head.

"She's perfect." I whisper reverently, completely entranced by the fragile creature in my arms. I experience a surge of pride and a rush of protectiveness that will not work in her favor the older she gets and if I had one wish, it was that I had never missed a second of her life.

A wailing voice from the couch rings out, "I promise I cared for her."

Faith turns and stares at the woman who is the image of her sister and says in a calm voice, "Why?"

Miss. Hughes stares at her in surprise. "I don't understand."

"Why did you agree to keep my child from me? You knew what Reverend Peters was like. You willingly helped a monster."

Miss. Hughes shakes her head. "I did it to help my sister. She has always been in love with him. She would do anything for him, and she has done everything for him."

"What do you mean—has?"

Faith's voice is wrapped in steel and Miss. Hughes stares down at the floor.

"I'm not saying I agree with what they did, but they had their reasons."

"What reasons were they, Miss. Hughes?" Faith's voice is measured, but I can tell she's guarding her anger well.

"God's work. Important work that cannot be questioned by the likes of us."

"Do you believe that God wanted the reverend to kill his past wives?"

Purity gasps and the frightened woman says with a tremble to her voice. "Augusta told me they were weak. Spineless and unable to withstand the devil within them. They took the easy way out, despite what my sister and the reverend did to help their poor souls."

The two men on either side of her turn and stare at her in disbelief and one of them says incredulously, "Fuck me, are you people really that fucking dumb?"

The other guy shakes his head. "Surely you don't believe that, darlin'? You're a schoolteacher. You must know right from wrong."

For the first time, Miss. Hughes looks worried and I can see her mind calculating what's been said.

"But they said it was God's work."

I gaze down at my innocent daughter and can't imagine the pain I would experience if she was hurt in any way, and I would do anything to protect her. It makes me think of my own parents and the way they eagerly gave me to a tyrant, knowing he would hurt me. It's an incredible pain inside knowing my parents thought more of the reverend and his lies than the bond they should have had for their only child. It sickens me. Miss. Hughes sickens me and the whole fucking town sickens me.

I stare with interest as Purity steps forward and looks like an angel, as she says with a fury that makes me smile.

"I pity you, Miss. Hughes." She says loudly, causing the bikers to grin widely.

"You are old enough to tell right from wrong, so shame on you. You care for other people's kids all day long and think it's ok to beat and torture the defenseless. You make me sick, and I am going to make it my business to report you to the authorities. And as for stealing a baby, you can face jail for that."

Rosemary stares at Purity as if she's seen an alien and the pretty girl steps beside Faith and says sternly, "If I were you, I would start talking. When the cops arrive, you tell them everything and leave nothing out, even if it sends your sister down for life. That is the only way you can make amends because if you don't, I'll make it my life's work to see that you pay. Got it, Miss. Hughes? Do you understand that because I'm a little concerned you don't know shit?"

The guys burst out laughing and Faith catches my eye and grins as Miss Hughes nods emphatically. "I'll do what's right. You can be assured of that."

Stepping forward, I cast another look at the baby who has made me a believer of love at first sight and reluctantly hand her to Faith and jerk my head toward the guys.

"Let's go home."

I glance at Purity and say with a grateful smile, "You coming, darlin?"

Faith nods emphatically. "Please, Purity. Come with us. We'll make sure you're ok. You don't have to go back."

Purity smiles sweetly with a flash of excitement in her eyes.

"I'm not going back, Faith. This is my get out of Heaven ticket and I'm cashing it in, and I have a place to go."

"Where?"

Faith says and Purity replies, "I want to head for Chicago. I have business there."

"Business?" Faith shakes her head in confusion. "What business and how do you know anyone in Chicago?"

Purity shrugs. "I have my ambitions, Faith. I always told myself if I ever left Heaven, I would try my luck in Chicago."

"But how? You have no money, nowhere to live, no friends …"

Faith breaks off as Purity holds up her hand and says with the determination that I am beginning to love about her, "I have my plan and I have money and for your information, I am assured of a place to stay."

"Tell me."

Faith won't give it up and Purity shrugs. "I can't say. I've kept this secret for many years and it's up to me to see it through."

Rebel steps forward and holds out his phone to Purity and Danny hands her a wad of dollar bills and a credit card. Rebel says firmly, "Just call home if you need us. It's programmed in and we'll be right there."

Danny says with a smile. "You've got balls, darlin', Chicago won't know what hit it."

Rebel steps forward and says, "I'll make sure she's ok."

Faith is agitated. "This isn't right. Purity, please. You're not strong enough to go there on your own."

"I won't be on my own."

This makes us all stare at her in surprise and she grins.

"I'll tell you all everything if it works out."

I watch as she hugs Faith carefully so as not to disturb Hope and she whispers, "I know where you are. If it doesn't work out, I'll come and find you. Pinky promise."

"Pinky promise." Faith says through her tears and Rebel says loudly, "Come on, darlin'. I'll take you to the airport and buy your ticket."

Her eyes light up and if she has any misgivings, she's hiding them well and as she heads to the door, she turns and fixes me with a frown. "Take care of my bestie and my god daughter or I'll be coming for you."

"So, she's your god daughter now." I grin and she shrugs. "Obviously. Who else would love that baby as much as I do outside of her own parents? I'll do anything for them, so watch your step, soldier."

She turns and Danny shakes his head as they leave the room and whistles, "Should I follow them?"

"Why?" Faith is worried, and he chuckles softly.

"I'm not sure Rebel is man enough to handle a woman like Purity."

"You've got that right." I laugh out loud and as I reach for Faith's hand, I can't get my family home quickly enough.

CHAPTER 23

FAITH

*M*r. Gaston is waiting and as we leave, Miss. Hughes, I say to Jonny, "What will happen to her?"

"The cops will pay her a visit. If they discover she was in on it, she can say goodbye to her freedom."

"Do you think she was?" I feel sick at the thought, and Jonny shrugs. "I doubt it. I'm guessing she was just believing everything her sister told her. That's the thing about our hometown, Faith. It's filled with gullible fools who can't think for themselves."

"Aside from a few." I smile as I gaze down at Hope and any worries instantly evaporate.

Arthur says over his shoulder. "I'm glad it worked out for you both, although God knows what I'm going to tell Purity's folks."

"Tell them nothing. I doubt they deserve it and if she wants them to know, she'll inform them herself." I say quickly, and Jonny nods in agreement.

"Her father worked for the reverend and is equally guilty.

I'm guessing he will be heading to jail, anyway. He was in too deep and who knows what he did to earn his place by Reverend Peter's side?"

I peer at him anxiously. "The reverend. What will happen about that? He's dead."

I am so worried because it's obvious Jonny killed him. I saw it in his eyes when he stepped from the church, but Jonny merely shrugs.

"He took the coward's way out. His wives' deaths will be investigated and when they discover he was a serial killer, nobody will care how he died, just that he did."

Arthur says angrily, "You got that right. I knew he was trouble, and my one regret is that I did nothing about it."

"You did enough." Jonny says kindly and as we fall silent, I notice that the car has reached an airfield where a shiny jet is patiently waiting.

"Where are we?" I say in confusion, and Jonny grins.

"I told you. Home."

"In that?" I'm amazed and excited because I have never been on a plane before.

"Yes. This aircraft belongs to the Reapers."

"You have your own plane. Bikers are that rich?" I say incredulously, and Arthur whistles. "Man, toss me some leathers and fire up a Harley. I'm in."

Jonny bursts out laughing.

"Anytime, Arthur. Just give me your size."

I stare in awe as the aircraft is surrounded by tattooed bikers, dripping in leather and banter. Their bikes are being loaded in the cargo hold and I feel the nerves shaking my fear back in place.

I stare down at my daughter and wonder what to do. This is no place for a child. Not surrounded by testosterone and men who kill for a living. I'm in no doubt about that because

I've witnessed it first-hand, and that's the man I'm heading there with.

Suddenly, Heaven is looking like a better proposition, and I hate myself for that. Surely, I'm safe with Jonny, aren't I? Aren't we?

Jonny has become a memory that has grown in importance in my life. I love him but am I *in* love with him? Would I knowingly put my daughter's well-being behind my own? How will this work and yet how can I stop it?

As we step outside the safety of the car, I'm edging toward staying right where I am and asking Mr. Gaston to drive me home. Perhaps he will let us stay with him. That could work, couldn't it?

I grip on tighter to Hope and fluctuate between doing what I think is right to what my heart wants.

I stare at Jonny as he hugs Mr. Gaston and I swear every part of me wants him. But is it enough?

Jonny steps back and throws me such a loving look, it brings tears to my eyes. He appears happy he has a daughter, but is this fair to expect him to take us both on? He was a single man when he came back into my life because I made it that way. Why is he even trying? It must be for Hope.

Mr. Gaston smiles at me with an encouragement I really need right now and as he steps into his car, I'm on a knife edge. One word is all that's needed. Tell him to stop, or to wait. I'm not ready for this. I'm a coward, and nothing like my best friend who couldn't wait to leave with a stranger.

"Breathe, Faith." Jonny slings his arm around my shoulder and whispers, "Trust me, darlin'. Please, for once in your life, trust me."

It's like a cool jet of water on an inferno, bringing calm and clarity to a volatile situation and, with a deep breath, I smile at him shakily. "Okay."

He leans down and presses a light kiss on my lips and the

memories that spark remind me of how good we were together. Good until I ruined everything and ran away from him. I want to run now, so badly, but this time I have no choice but to face my fear and trust him. That's what he said, and I need to believe I can. Surely, wherever we're going can't be worse than Heaven. Can it?

The aircraft makes me stare in wonder as we step inside, and I see rows of seats set in lines. There also appears to be a communal area and as we pass through, I see a small kitchen.

Jonny explains, "We use the plane to move around the country. I'll tell you why another time, but first we need to settle in. When Ryder gets here, it won't be long before we're airborne."

"Is he your boss?" I say in awe, and he grins.

"He's our president and yes, that also means boss in our world. He's our commanding officer and we go against him at our peril. He calls the shots, and you will be in the safest hands in the world when you are under his wing."

He nods to the men; all ripping rings off beer cans as they chat loudly and rolls his eyes.

"You get used to them. They are rough and loud but have golden hearts. They are loyal soldiers who need to let off steam occasionally."

I smile, but inside my stomach is churning. It's so overpowering I can't think straight. Jonny alone is overpowering. He always was a force of nature that carried me along with him until I fell hard. He was everything to me. An exotic species that captured my attention and ran away with my heart. I followed him into madness, and it was the hardest thing I ever did to run from him, knowing I was carrying our baby. I did it for him, not for me. At least that's what I told myself.

Now I'm faced with the consequences of my actions, I'm

uncertain what the future holds but it's a scary one. I'm not sure I'm strong enough and I hate that I'm already planning my escape.

CHAPTER 24

JONNY

*A*s soon as Ryder steps on board with the rest of the Reapers, the doors close and the engines start, and I breathe a deep sigh of relief.

Thank God. She can't back out now.

I realize she's scared. I can tell she's having a panic attack inside and the only reason she's not freaking out right now is because she has Hope to care for. I watch as she straps her in along with herself and holds her tightly, nuzzling her little head and planting sweet kisses on her cheeks.

Nothing prepared me for how emotional this would be. I have a family. An instant family that I didn't even know about.

As the bird soars into the sky, I reach for Faith's hand and smile at her with a reassurance I really hope she believes. She is nervous and doesn't appear to want to say much, so as soon as the plane levels out, I excuse myself and head to debrief with Ryder, Snake and Brewer.

They are sitting in the communal area and as I drop down in the seat beside Brewer, he chucks me a beer.

"You look like you need this. How's the family?"

He raises his eyes in concern and I sigh. "As good as can be expected. This is a lot for Faith to wrap her head around."

Ryder appears thoughtful. "How are you, Jonny?"

"Worried." I frown and take a gulp of my beer.

"She ran from me once and when she sees where we're heading, I doubt she'll stick around long."

"Leave it with me."

Ryder turns to Snake. "The girls can take it from here."

I smile gratefully. "Will they be ok with that?"

"Of course." Snake looks concerned. "We aren't the ones to make your lady feel at home. We're scary motherfuckers who will never be anything else, and it's fortunate we live among angels who won't let us down. Leave Faith with Ashton and Bonnie. They'll reassure her. They're good at that."

I catch Ryder's eye and he nods. "I haven't met a woman yet who doesn't change her mind after they get working on them."

He turns to Brewer. "What about accommodation? She can't stay in the block."

Brewer says thoughtfully, "The house near Maverick's is almost complete. Just needs some paint and the kitchen finishing off."

"Who was moving in?" Snake asks, and Ryder shakes his head. "Nobody. Tiger had his name on it but crashed and burned."

The guys laugh and I join them. Tiger was so sure his childhood sweetheart was going to say 'yes' when he asked her to marry him. He didn't count on her ambition though, and she turned him down and moved to Seattle instead, where she had been offered a high-powered job. To say he was pissed was putting it lightly, and he has spent every night since then fucking around just to erase her from his memory.

"Then it's settled." Ryder says as he cracks open a can

himself. "Jonny and Faith can move in with Hope." He raises his can in my direction. "Good luck, soldier. Instant families are hard to adjust to. I should know."

The guys laugh because we all remember what happened when Ashton walked into the Rubicon. There was no way in hell Ryder was going to let her stay anywhere but with him. It was instant attraction that brought out the bastard in him, and he used every trick in the book to win her heart.

I just hope I have his skill set because my own battle is just beginning, which is sure to be a hard one.

For the next hour, we debrief the mission and I wonder if Ryder knew what was happening there all along. He was the one who insisted I went and as they wrap it up, I say, "Out of curiosity. Did you send me there because of the reverend? Did you know about this?"

Ryder glances at Snake and they smile. "I heard a whisper." He shrugs. "I figured you had business there and decided to give you a helping hand. It worked out well for everyone."

He nods and then as I reach out, his expression softens as I shake his hand and say gratefully, "Thanks for being the bastard I needed to set my mind straight."

"Anytime, soldier." He winks, and I doubt this man will ever stop surprising me. He has it all worked out, and I'm in awe of him. Ryder King is a living legend and I'm the lucky one who gets to witness that first-hand.

When I make my way back to Faith, she is sleeping. They both are, and I take a moment to stare at the beauty before me. Faith was always a stunner. Even as a child, I realized that. She was a pretty little thing with dark, naturally curly hair, the tawny highlights that caught the sun, marking her out as different somehow. Her amazing aquamarine eyes couldn't decide if they preferred to be blue or green, so settled for an unusual color in between.

Her beauty attracted me, but her personality made me fall —hard because Faith, as it turned out, was a force of nature I had never seen the like of before. She was adventurous, a little wild, and cheeky. It was hidden behind a protective wall of shyness that was adorable and brought out the protector in me.

When we first met, she was in awe of me. It was obvious. I had a reputation and most of the folks in the town couldn't figure me out at all. They didn't trust me. The devil boy. I heard them whisper it when I was coming and some even said it to my face. It stemmed from my visit to the good reverend. My own parents created the stigma when they punished me for being a small, unruly child.

Subsequently, I grew into an unruly teenager, angry with them—with the world. My world was Heaven then, and it was only when I used to watch the delivery trucks disappearing out of town did I dare to imagine there was another life out there.

I took my chance one day and never looked back and when I returned, I discovered nothing much had changed except for one thing. One person and I'm looking at her now because on the fateful day I bumped into Faith, my life changed forever.

She stirs and a small smile graces her soft plump lips, and my body reacts to her as it probably always will. She appears so fragile, and yet when we're together, it's as if an electric storm is lighting up the heavens. I wonder if that still exists. Will she even want me in that way?

The doubt in her eyes is hard to see. She ran from me because of something I did. Possibly believing the rumors and deciding I wasn't worth the trouble. I knocked her up. I was the orchestrator of her downfall and I'm guessing there weren't a lot of people in town who congratulated her on her good fortune.

As I sit beside her, I physically ache to lift her hand and bring it to my lips. To hold her, to comfort her and to love her. To be a team, a partnership and, when our beautiful daughter is sleeping, to be the lover she deserves.

Instead, I take advantage of her dreaming. To stare at her without interruption and marvel that she even gave me the time of day. Together we created perfection and as I stare in awe at my beautiful daughter sleeping peacefully in her arms, something stirs inside me that feels a lot like love, devotion, and adoration.

My entire world sleeps in an airline seat and I am unsure how to make them want to stay.

CHAPTER 25

FAITH

I wake up as the engine noise changes. It pulls me from my dreams that I wish were reality.

In them, we are a normal family. Jonny, Hope and me. Living by the sea in a white house set on a cliff edge. Hope played on the beach and was happy. We were happy, and Jonny was the best husband I could ever wish for.

As I crash back to reality, I wake to a huge problem because I am not in my dream. I am in my worst nightmare. The only saving grace is that they are in it with me because, despite everything, I wouldn't want to be anywhere else.

I blink my fear away and turn to see Jonny staring at me with an intensity that takes my breath away and, as always, when I look at him, a shiver of excitement passes through me.

How did I get so lucky? How did I get so unlucky at the same time?

I am so afraid for Hope, me and Jonny, because we have been thrust together through circumstance and I am so worried he is only doing the right thing by us. He has moved on. I pushed him away and now he is dealing with a whole pile of shit because of me.

He killed a man. One of many, so I believe, and I don't know how he can live with that. Make no mistake, Reverend Peters deserved everything coming to him but to take another man's life – any life, goes against everything I grew up with. I hate how that impressed me deep down. How I cheered for him and delighted in the reverend's passing. It makes me a sinner just like Jonny, and that worries me more than anything.

"Hey, gorgeous." His husky voice makes desire wrap me in the urgent need to be as close as we once were. To enjoy the slide of his skin against mine. Soft touches and hard kisses. The familiarity of lovers with the excitement of strangers meeting and the unknown. Jonny always did throw a grenade into my world, which is ironic when a grenade blew up my life back there. Like the one that rolled down the aisle in the church, I am waiting for it to go off and I just hope the explosion doesn't kill me in the end. It will wreak havoc; I already know that and so the urge to run away from it is so strong I hate myself.

"We're coming in to land. We'll soon be home." His husky voice breaks my thoughts.

"Is it far?"

I'm nervous and it must show as he reaches across, and I hate that he hesitates before dropping his hand on Hope's sleeping little head. He touches her with a reverence that makes my soul weep. She is a stranger to him, an unwanted burden perhaps, but even now he looks at her as if she is the most precious thing in the world. The way he looks at me. The way he has *always* looked at me.

"You have nothing to fear, despite what the people of Heaven have told you."

"What's it like?"

I'm intrigued and encouraged when his face lights up as he thinks about the place he calls home.

"It's different. I won't pretend otherwise, but when you get over the shock, you realize it's the perfect place to live. It's full of strong men and women who are fierce in their love of our ways. They are free, Faith. Freedom is something the Rubicon encourages and offers in bucket loads. The Reapers encourage you to be strong, fearless and brave and reward you well for it. They drag your soul out into the light and build you into a better person and inside those walls, you can be anything you want to be."

"It sounds…" I hesitate because on the one hand, it sounds like paradise, but I'm scared of the people who live there. They have been undoubtedly kind but I'm not like them. But Jonny is. He is *exactly* like them, and I fell in love with him before he wore the jacket of death and sharpened his rough edges. He was a soldier, not a biker, and I'm still struggling to understand that.

"I'm still the same man I always was."

His gentle voice calms my raging spirit and I wonder how he reads my mind so well. He always has, and he once told me it was like reading an open book when he stared into my eyes, and I guess that's the truth. He always did know what I was thinking and so I smile bravely as Hope stirs in my arms. "I think she's hungry."

The panic on Jonny's face almost makes me laugh and I say shyly, "It's ok, I have everything I need provided by Mother Nature, except privacy perhaps."

The realization dawns in his eyes and he makes to move and, reaching out, I place my hand on his arm and say shyly, "Stay. I won't mind. Unless you'd rather not, that is."

Once again, I'm nervous because despite the small human

between us that we created, Jonny is still a stranger to me now. The yearning in his eyes undoes me a little as he nods and smiles, striking me like a dart in the heart. He always was the most handsome boy in Heaven, and I could deny him nothing but when Jonny gazes at me like he is now, I would tear out my heart and offer it to him every single time because he always did have the ability to take my breath away.

The fact we're alone up here, the other men some distance behind, makes this easy and as I pull Hope to my breast, I love the bond that always brings with it. I feel a little self-conscious with Jonny beside me, but I don't want to deny him any of the experiences a young baby brings.

"Does it hurt?"

He sounds concerned and I laugh softly, "It hurts knowing that one day soon I won't be enough for her. That she will need something more than I can give her."

He watches in fascination as she feeds and I whisper, "I want to be the best mother I can be. I want to give her everything I ever wished for, along with her own. I want to be her wish fairy and raise her to be strong and brave. Like her father."

His eyes leave Hope and stare deep into mine, and what I see in them makes my breath hitch. There he is, the man I fell in love with, desperately trying to disguise the boy he once was. To be a man, to be a warrior, but floundering as he tries to adjust to being a father.

"Like her mother." He reassures me and I say a little sadly. "I don't feel strong right now."

I peer at the ridiculous dress I'm traveling in and sigh. "What will they think when I roll up in this monstrosity? It's as if I'm wearing sackcloth and ashes and what must I look like."

I gingerly touch the still throbbing bruises on my face and Jonny leans closer and whispers, "You have never looked more beautiful to me."

"Have you got shit in your eyes?" I make a joke to break the intensity of the moment because I am shy about dealing with it. It's one thing remembering what it was like lying with Jonny, but another thing entirely knowing that he will probably expect me to pick up where we left off.

I want him, hell I crave him. So much it hurts, but I'm nervous. What if I'm no longer good enough? He must have slept with countless women since I ran away. I wouldn't blame him; I *don't* blame him. Why would he settle for a naive girl from Heaven when he has grown up and sampled much better than me?

"The only woman I have ever had standing behind my eyes is you, Faith."

He says it simply and directly and it stuns me a little. He leans forward and whispers, "I don't want to scare you darlin', but I am trying real hard to be a gentleman here. To do the right thing and not to scare you off again. Something happened back in time to cause you to fear me, and I don't want to make the same mistake twice. I want to kiss you so badly, to wrap you in my arms and hold on tight. To love you, to make you love me, but something is telling me you're not ready for that. So, I'll wait until you are and if you never are, I will accept your wishes, knowing I have failed in securing the only person I have ever loved. You."

"Kiss me, Jonny."

My eyes flash with a determination I never really knew was there because right now, in this moment, that is the only thing I want from life.

As his lips press gently over mine, a huge wave of relief hits me hard. There he is, there's my man and suddenly the future doesn't seem so frightening anymore.

As kisses go it's more of a promise. A soft, sensual promise of what will happen when the dust settles. It reassures my mind and fills my heart and I suppose I've always known that with Jonny beside me, I am invincible.

CHAPTER 26

JONNY

I am trying so hard to tread carefully with Faith, but it's an impossible task. Not when she scrambles my mind and plays with my emotions. I have tried so hard to get over her and yet one glimpse was all it took to bring me right back where I started.

Now I must keep her and I'm not sure she will allow that to happen, so what happens next will be the making or breaking of my family.

If she runs again, I'm not sure I'm strong enough to chase her. My pride got in the way the first time, but how many times can a man try before admitting defeat?

As the guys exit the aircraft, I know she is nervous and, as Ryder stops by on his way, he stares at her with concern.

"You ok, darlin'?" His husky drawl is strangely caring, and she smiles tightly, looking anything but ok.

"I'm fine. Thank you for asking." She says politely, and he smiles as he nods. "One of the guys has brought a car to take you all home. There will be a car seat in the back, and you will find everything you need waiting at the house we've stamped your name on."

"A house." Faith's eyes are wide because I doubt she expected that, and Ryder nods. "The families live in houses we build out the back of the compound. You will find many women eager to make friends and tons of kids who can't wait to welcome a new one."

"You make it sound so…" She falters and blushes as I add, "Normal?" Ryder grins as she nods, a little embarrassed.

"The Reapers may be a club filled with bikers, but we are also a community. The guys are just part of that, and you will find many women only too happy to talk to you about life there. My wife Ashton will be waiting to offer a warm welcome, along with Bonnie, Snake's much better half."

The man himself heads our way and rasps, "I heard that." He turns to Faith and winks. "You'll soon see why Bonnie stays. She adores every bad bone in my body."

"Keep telling yourself that and one day you may even believe it."

Ryder shakes his head. "If you have any questions, ask the girls. If they can't answer them, ask Sinner and if he gives you any trouble, you come to me."

I say fiercely, "She won't have any problems with me. You can be sure of that."

Faith laughs softly as the two guys wink and head toward the door, and I say softly, "I wouldn't bring you here if I didn't think it was the best place possible for you and Hope. As I said before, just trust me sweetheart, I only want what's best for you."

I stand and hold out my arms to take Hope from her, so she can organize herself before we head outside. As my daughter snuggles against me, I love hearing her soft breath against my ear. She feels as light as a feather and as fragile and is obviously an angel because she has not complained once in all the time I've known her. The fact I wasn't there when she was born is something I must let go because I'm here now and intend on treating them both so well they will never want to leave.

* * *

BLADE IS WAITING and I curse the fact he was sent at all. He's not a great advert for my cause because he is one scary motherfucker. We call him Blade because he wears a six-inch scar down his right cheek, and he loves to wear a bandana around his shoulder length hair that is currently tied in a ponytail around the back. His dark unshaven jaw is brooding and rarely smiling and his eyes flash with animosity even when he is. He is larger than most of the Reapers, courtesy of his insane height and triceps that could wrestle a bear. Blade is not the best walking advert for normality, and I sense Faith stiffen as I whisper, "This is as bad as it gets, Faith. Underneath it all, he's a pussycat."

Faith colors up when he nods and throws his cigarette to the ground, stamping on it hard.

"Welcome, darlin'." He growls in a deep voice that I liken to rusty nails on a chalk board. Rough, unrefined, and crude, much like the man himself, and I'm wondering if this is a shock tactic because nothing at the Rubicon will be as bad as him.

"Hi." Faith says shyly and I almost detect a gleam of humor in Blade's eye as he peers at my daughter.

"What's her name?" he says, jerking his thumb to the bundle in Faith's arms and she says shakily, "Hope."

He grins, revealing a strangely perfect set of white teeth and says more gently than I have ever heard him speak, "She's a beauty." He flicks his gaze at me and shakes his head.

"What?" I say scratchily and he grins. "She sure doesn't take after you, Sinner. How the fuck did you create something so perfect?"

From the expression on Faith's face, she is already happier than when we met him, and I sense myself relaxing. Yes, sending Blade was a stroke of genius and whoever's idea it was, has earned my undying gratitude.

Once they are settled in the car, I sit beside Blade and join the line of Harleys, all heading in one direction. My own bike has been loaded on a separate truck, along with our baggage and despite how much I love riding with my brothers, riding with my family tops it every single time.

"I heard the mission was a success." Blade makes conversation and I nod, glad to be away from that fucking town.

"You could say that."

I look behind me and am rewarded with the sweetest smile from two angels, and it makes my heart lurch when I witness the desire flashing in Faith's eyes. I know that look. I've seen it countless times before and I didn't really expect to see it again. As we lock eyes, there is a stirring in my pants that tells me only one thing. Tonight is going to be a bastard if she doesn't feel the same.

Hope is awake and smiling as Faith tickles her under the chin and holds her little hand as she plays with her fingers. I can't tear my eyes from them because this is like a hammer delivering blows to my heart.

This is everything to me and I steal many a glance in the rear-view mirror and hope like crazy everything works out for us.

Blade turns on the radio and sweet country music fills the car and I tease, "I didn't have you down as a country boy, Blade."

"It was my grandma's favorite. Dolly Parton was her idol, and I grew up on it." He shrugs. "It has its place, but I prefer heavy rock, if I'm honest."

It makes me laugh because why am I not surprised?

"I was in a band once." He says suddenly.

"What happened?" I'm interested because Blade doesn't open up much about life before the Reapers and he shrugs. "The usual shit. Manager got greedy. The rest of the band pissed away our fortune on drugs and whores and we ended up in a blackmail plot to expose us to the press."

"Yeah, usual shit." I shake my head as Faith giggles, and I say with interest. "What was the band called?"

"Hell." He says with a shrug, and I catch Faith's eye and we share an amused grin.

"What happened after Hell froze over?" I joke and he sighs. "Things were hot for a while, so I enlisted. Didn't take long to reach the marines and after an unfortunate altercation with my commanding officer, I was sent to Ryder."

He sighs heavily. "Fucking disgrace."

He growls, "I was dishonorably discharged because I took no shit from him, when he was the one servicing whores and dealing in drugs."

I shift in my seat as he laughs out loud. "I got the last laugh, though. He fucked up and after an anonymous tip off, found himself court martialled and is currently serving ten in the penitentiary. Word is, it's not going well."

Faith catches my eye and I smile and am happy to receive one in return. Blade's story is just one of many similar ones at the Rubicon, but that isn't what worries me. It's what happens in the bar that concerns me because it's definitely not a place for an innocent like Faith and I wonder how she'll react when she sees exactly how I've been spending my time since she's been gone.

CHAPTER 27

FAITH

*D*espite his appearance, I've taken quite a liking to Blade. Like Jonny said, he hides a heart of gold under that insane body, and I wonder if he has a family where we're heading. I wouldn't dare ask, though. In fact, the less I say, the better because I don't want to draw anyone's attention onto me. They scare the shit out of me, and yet when I see Jonny sitting beside the rugged biker, he doesn't look as out of place as I figured he would.

Since I left, he's grown a little rougher, stronger even, and the body he wears like a suit designed to trap a woman's soul is all I can focus on right now.

We have a house. We are a family. I am still wrapping my head around that, and as we turn off the highway onto a side road, my heart lurches when I consider what happens next.

The guys chat about people I've never heard of and I'm glad to be left alone with my thoughts. I study the passing scenery and note civilization left us a while back, the smart houses giving way to open countryside and as the cavalcade slows down, I watch with growing interest where they're heading.

We turn off onto a dirt track that appears to lead absolutely nowhere. There is no indication there is anything here at all and as we pass trees, large bushes and dilapidated structures, my heart is in my mouth as I struggle to drag some bravery out from somewhere.

I stare with growing trepidation as the bikes all stop outside a huge steel building. The bikers, jeering as they rile each other up. The chrome from the handlebars gleaming in the diminishing light when night steals the day away.

My eyes widen at the sheer size of the steel compound as they call it and I stare at the huge sign that hangs above the door.

Abandon hope all who enter here.

I stare at my daughter with a wry smile. There will be no abandoning of hope all the time I breathe and so as we pull to a stop, I dig deep for the bravery my daughter needs from me.

Blade turns off the ignition and spins around, his dark eyes twinkling as they stare at me hard. "I'll say this only once, darlin'."

I swear I hold my breath because I couldn't move if I wanted to, and he growls, "If you have any trouble from anyone inside these walls, you come and find me if Jonny ain't around. I want sunshine and rainbows with a few unicorns thrown in where you're concerned, and I'll accept nothing less."

Jonny rolls his eyes, but I can see why he loves these guys so much. Not a single one of them to this point hasn't made me extremely welcome and set my mind at rest.

"Thanks, Blade." I whisper shyly, his name sounding strange as it falls from my lips, and he nods.

"Then don't keep the president's old lady waiting. She's looking mighty anxious over there."

I turn and see an extremely pretty woman standing beside her husband, peering anxiously in our direction, and I stare in fascination as he leans down and whispers something in her ear that makes her bat his hand away. He laughs, and it's obvious they have an easy relationship, which makes me feel a lot better.

I watch as another woman with bright red hair runs up to join her and the scary snake man heads across and swings her into his gigantic arms. She throws her head back and laughs and for some reason, it makes me smile. They are happy. It's obvious and so I don't feel quite as bad as I thought I would as Jonny helps us from the car.

The group head our way and the president's old lady, as they call her, says with a huge smile, "Hiya, honey, welcome to the Rubicon. Take no notice of the name. I'm trying to get Ryder to agree to change it to Happiness House."

He rolls his eyes as the guys jeer and she drops me a cheeky wink as the other girl surges forward. "I'm Bonnie and I'm so pleased to meet you, honey. Now let me take a look at that adorable baby gurgling in your arms."

Jonny slaps his arm around my shoulder, and I don't miss the fond looks the women direct his way as they say happily, "Your daughter is beautiful, Jonny. Then again..." Ashton says. "Faith is every bit as gorgeous as you told us she was."

I stare at Jonny in surprise, and he shrugs, "Don't be surprised, darlin'. Everyone has a past in The Rubicon and it gets dragged out you pretty darned quickly when you join up."

Ryder grins and then says loudly, "We should let the girls settle Faith and Hope in. Jonny, as much as it will be like tearing the skin from your back, you should come and grab a beer and leave the women to it."

I study Jonny's reaction and as he hesitates, I say softly, "It's ok. Go and grab a beer. You must need one after the day we've had."

He appears anxious and hovers uncertainly as the other men head to the large front door and Bonnie snaps, "Just fuck off, Sinner. We've got this."

I'm amazed when he merely grins and steals a quick kiss from me and presses one on Hope's soft head before he heads after the guys, leaving me with two women who couldn't have been nicer.

"Thank God they've gone." Ashton rolls her eyes. "We love them all to death, but they're so overpowering at times. Especially after a mission."

Bonnie nods. "You'll get used to it, Faith. It's a pretty scary place the first time you set eyes on it, but you soon realize its paradise."

Ashton smiles sweetly, "Come on. I'm dying to show you your house. We've been getting it ready ever since we learned you were moving in."

Bonnie nods as she falls into step beside me.

"I love designing interiors and I've made this super special for you. I didn't have long, but I enjoyed maxing out Snake's credit card to fix your darlin' baby's room up. Just wait until you see it. I'm pretty pleased about this one."

Ashton whispers behind her hand. "She's practicing ready for her own."

"You're pregnant?" I say with a huge smile, and she shakes her head. "Not yet, but I'm working god-damned hard on making one."

She grins an impudent grin and Ashton giggles. "You'll get used to Snake and Bonnie, Faith. They can't keep their hands off one another. It won't be long."

Ashton carries on without drawing breath. "I have two

children. Cassie, our darlin' daughter, and Caspian, our little prince."

Bonnie's eyes soften. "You'll love them, Faith. So cute and sooo naughty. Well, Cassie is anyway. Caspian's still figuring it all out and is more controllable because he can't even walk yet."

Ashton smiles fondly. "Seeing little Hope here has made me god-damned broody again. Just don't tell Ryder, because I'll be knocked up before you finish your sentence."

The two women laugh out loud, and I wonder if I'll ever fit in. Speaking about such things was forbidden in Heaven and yet they speak of sex like they're discussing the weather.

I follow the two women around the back of the large steel building and Ashton points to two blocks that sit on either side of the path.

"Those are the blocks that the single Reapers live in. Boys in one and girls in the other."

"You have women as Reapers?" I'm shocked and then the awkward silence tells me I've misunderstood.

Bonnie says quickly, "Listen, Faith, there's something you should know, and it's not half as bad as it sounds."

"What?" I'm a little uneasy and Bonnie adds, "The girls aren't Reapers, honey, they're Reaper whores."

I stare at her in total shock and feel a growing sense of unease building.

Ashton says quickly, "It's just a word, honey, and doesn't mean what you think it does. The girls chose the name themselves and they work in the bar and around the compound until they're ready to move on."

Bonnie adds quickly, "While they're here, they enjoy the company of the single guys. Not exclusively, just who they fancy hooking up with for the night. Sometimes they catch feelings, but more often the whores decide to move on and carry on the lives that were interrupted when they came here to start again."

"We all did," Ashton says sadly. "There is not one person here who hasn't faced a hard beginning, me included."

"You were a…" I can't bring myself to say the word, and Ashton shakes her head with a smile.

"No. I came here as Cassie's nanny. Ryder was a single daddy and needed help and, well, I was looking for a place to hide and my brother arranged it."

"But you were expected to…" Again, I falter because I can't process what I'm hearing.

Ashton grins. "No. Ryder took one look at me and told me I was no longer required as a nanny."

Bonnie laughs out loud. "He married the poor girl."

"And you agreed?" I'm astonished and Ashton blushes a pretty shade of pink.

"I was so angry and fearful, much like you, and this place scared the shit out of me. Ryder told me he could only guarantee my safety if I was his old lady and, like a fool, I believed him."

"He was lying?" My eyes are wide because how many more sins can a person learn of before they burn in hell and this time Ashton laughs out loud. "To an extent, but I didn't know that. I just saw the whores and the way they were dressed, and the bastard made sure I was seeing the compound at its worst. I agreed on the condition I had my own room, and it was in name only."

Bonnie says drily, "You can see how well it worked."

She rolls her eyes. "It didn't take long either. Ashton says *we* can't keep our hands off each other. Well, ditto baby, with more besides. Ashton broke several hearts the day she married Ryder and I'm guessing there were a few bikers none too pleased, either."

We reach an area where normal looking houses form a

street of sorts and I note the pretty white wooden paint and roses climbing around the door. There are white picket fences and a clean and tidy lawn out front, and I gasp, "What is this place?"

"It's where the families live. The old ladies and the kids."

Bonnie explains, "Old Lady means wife in Biker speak. Both Ashton and me are old ladies and you will be too if you marry, Sinner."

Marry Jonny! For some reason, that makes my heart flutter because I never believed Jonny would want to marry me. That I would be eating his dust if he ever found out I was pregnant. Now I feel like a fool and as we stop outside a freshly painted house, the tears in my eyes are telling me that I hope he has enough forgiveness in his heart for me because it immediately feels as if I'm coming home.

CHAPTER 28

JONNY

*W*e meet in Ryder's office, and as I head inside, Brewer chucks me a beer. "Take a seat, Jonny." He says, shifting on the couch. Ryder is sitting behind his desk with his feet on it, his chair angled back while he holds a beer. Snake is leaning forward on his seat by the wall, dangling the beer between his legs, and I'm instantly aware this isn't a casual debrief. There is something super-charging the atmosphere and I don't like it at all.

"We need to talk about the Dark Lords."

I figured he'd want to debrief on the last mission they sent me on because I went straight to Heaven from the mafia mansion I was undercover in.

"What do you want to know?"

I take a swig of the cool beer and Ryder drawls, "We are all aware the Ortegas were caught up in that shit courtesy of Matasso and his son Mario. You would hope that following their deaths, the Dark Lord's shit died with them."

"Part of it, I'm guessing, but they were a small branch of that organization." I add.

Ryder shrugs. "They ran their own sick society and called

it The Dark Lords. They were never part of the inner circle though, just hovering on the edge, waiting to be granted access."

"So, what are you saying?" I stare at him with interest, and he flicks a look at Snake who growls, "This just isn't going away. What's the plan?"

Ryder sets the bottle down and sighs. "When Baron asked me to send an operative, I figured it would be an in and out job. A one off even. He needed to settle an old debt and this Dark Lord's shit got in the way of that. I took a call from him while you were visiting your folks and he's concerned."

"Then it must be bad."

Snake whistles. "If Baron's concerned, something big is going down."

Ryder nods, tapping his finger on the desk, which is always a sign he's thinking hard. None of us interrupt him, and then he leans back and shakes his head. "Giselle Matasso is currently visiting her family before heading back to the Hamptons to begin her new life. A curious detour that has me wondering."

"Don Vieri?" Snake says with interest, and Ryder nods.

"Her grandfather started the Dark Lord's society when he was in high school. I doubt he even knew how powerful it would become and, like most beasts, it's turning on his successor."

"So, what're you saying?" Brewer is alert and taking everything in and Ryder shrugs. "I'm not certain, but word on the street is the Dark Lords want to clean up their act and having mafia involved isn't good for their respectability."

He fixes me with his usual dark glare.

"You worked for them. Did you discover anything that could help us?"

I consider it carefully because my mission was purely to infiltrate the Ortega family and watch events unfold and report back. I was assigned as a guard to Flora Corlietti. The woman Domenico Ortega fell in love with who was linked to Matasso and his son. She was innocent, but I watched the sick rituals that Mario carried out in the name of the Dark Lords and hoped it had ended with their deaths.

I tell them everything I know, which isn't much as it happens. However, when I get to the part where Jared Kensington arranged for his own daughter to head into the lion's den, Ryder sits up and takes notice.

"Jared Kensington." he says thoughtfully.

"Baron knows him well. His own daughter is now married to Matteo Ortega, which makes me wonder."

"Why distance your organization from mafia and yet marry your only daughter into it?" I add, and Ryder nods thoughtfully.

"It appears the mafia are fighting back. Word on the streets is the Vieris are pissed they are being side-lined by the billionaires. A hostile takeover of the organization that was founded by Don Vieri senior himself. This could get messy and hit the headlines because their membership includes some of the most wealthy and influential people in this great country. It's a scandal waiting to explode and all because they are now fighting among themselves."

"Why should that concern us?" Snake shrugs and Ryder leans forward, a hard glint in his eye. "Because one of their members pays our fucking wages and has ordered a stop to it. We have no choice but to discover what the fuck is going on, so I need someone on the inside."

I hold up my hands. "Sorry, Ryder, respectfully I must pass. I just found my family and I can't take off and leave them so soon."

"You've done your bit, Sinner. You are due some time out."

"Maverick?" Brewer adds. "His own brothers run the Romano mafia. He *is* mafia for Christ's sake."

"Who expressly told us when he patched in that he would do anything but mafia?"

"That worked well for him." Snake chuckles softly. "Considering the woman he married was a Moretti."

"He's perfect." Brewer adds, and Ryder shakes his head. "I must respect his wishes. I need someone else."

"Blade?" I say with a shrug. "He's certainly dangerous enough."

"Let me think on it." Ryder says with a sigh.

"Apparently, the current Don Vieri's health is deteriorating, and his son Benito is reluctant to leave his blue-chip business to take over from him."

"Who is in the running, then?" Brewer says with interest, and Ryder raises his eyes. "His grandson, Killian Vieri."

"So, problem solved, it skips a generation." Brewer replies.

"Possibly, but that doesn't solve the problem. It creates an even bigger one."

"Because…" Snake says, fixing him with a dark look.

"Because Killian Vieri was born to be a mafia don. He thrives on everything it represents and above all, he is a loyal family man and any talk of cutting the family out of The Dark Lords will be a battle cry."

"I see your point." Snake sighs. "Fucking mafia. You never know what shit is going down. Give me a biker any day."

We all laugh and raise our beers. "Amen to that."

Ryder looks my way and says with interest. "You've got a lot on your plate, Sinner. You should head off to settle your family in."

"But what about this Dark Lord's shit?"

"If you think of anything, you know where we are. We need to dwell on this a bit more because it won't be an easy one."

I nod, glad to be off the hook because hanging around with mafia really isn't my style at all.

As I leave the office, I wonder how Ryder does this day in and week out. He has a family of his own, a club of his own, and somehow, he manages to keep them both happy. I am facing a struggle of my own, and as I head toward the house set behind my room in the block, I know I will have a shit load of explaining to do when I get there.

CHAPTER 29

FAITH

I am blown away by this house. The minute I stepped inside, I fell in love. Coming from a home where minimalism was a way of life, this one is opulence on a grand scale.

Mainly it's open plan and I love the modern interior. There is so much light, even in the darkening light, it blinds me. The kitchen is brand new and appears modern and sleek and the huge island in the center makes me imagine an advert for a family commercial, where the kids all bake cookies with their mom, while the dog barks for scraps.

We never had the luxury of a television as it was considered useful only to men, but we knew where we could find one and when Roddy Hawkins left for work each day, Purity used to meet me there and we would sit and watch things that educated our minds far more than any school in Heaven.

As I gaze around me, I can tell it's a happy home and my jaw drops when I see the modern fire jump into life at the flick of a remote control. Comfortable couches sit before it and deep pile rugs offer soft comfort to walk on. Discreet lighting illuminates alcoves that I didn't even know were there. A large table is set before the huge sliding glass doors leading onto a yard which has raised decking holding two rocking chairs.

Bonnie and Ashton excitedly show me every modern convenience I have ever seen and when we reach the nursery, I can't prevent the tears from falling.

"Wait, what? Don't you like it." Bonnie says anxiously and I turn to her with my eyes lit with gratitude. "I love it. Really love it." I'm not kidding either because this is my dream nursery.

It's painted white with lights that resemble white fluffy clouds hanging from a ceiling that has been painted to resemble a pink sky. The walls are white but hold mirrors in the shape of clouds and hidden lighting that changes as Bonnie runs through a sequence on the remote. The white painted crib stands off center, with a huge pink fluffy rug resting on the white carpet. There are little white cupboards that, when opened, hold everything I could possibly need for Hope and an attached bathroom that is every girl's dream. Modern fixtures and luxurious accessories equip a luxurious room and there is even a changing station by the huge window overlooking the pretty yard.

A huge stuffed white bear sits in the corner of the bedroom and there is absolutely nothing I can find fault with.

Ashton says with excitement. "Come and look at your bedroom."

I follow her with Hope in my arms and wonder how I got so lucky. When I see the huge emperor-sized bed, I do a double take because my own bed at home was a twin.

"I'll get lost in there." I say with a giggle and Bonnie grins. "I doubt it. Those Reapers take up quite a bit of the space if yours is anything like mine."

I say nothing, but her words make me freeze. Of course. I am part of a family now and that means I sleep with Jonny.

I must be as white as one of Bonnie's fluffy clouds, because Ashton says with concern. "Are you ok, honey?"

"Of course." I force a bright smile on my face as the door slams downstairs and the two women stare at one another and grin.

"Our time is up." Bonnie says with a sigh.

"We'll drop by tomorrow and answer any more questions you have. Have a good evening."

They exchange an amused smile, but I'm not laughing. This is it. My Rubicon. My point of no return because the enormity of what I've agreed to is consuming every thought in my head.

Jonny is used to someone in his bed. It's obvious after what the women told me. He was a single man and probably enjoyed the company of many single ladies. If I don't play my part, he has a whole block of choices a stone's throw away.

Sex with Jonny is nothing new. When we first met, it was inevitable. I was infatuated with him. Curious and had been held on a leash for so long, the minute I saw my chance, I took it, and it was everything I hoped for. I was lit by desire and drunk on lust. We couldn't get enough of one another and just the memory makes me shiver with desire.

But that was ages ago, and a lot has happened since then. I'm no longer the sweet, naive girl he said he fell in love with. I'm the bitch who ran away with his child and never even gave him the right to know of her existence. He must hate me and just picturing lying beside him in that huge bed fills me with so much pain because how can it ever be the same again? Not after what I did to him.

Bonnie and Ashton are staring at me with concern, and I raise a half smile and stare down at my sleeping baby, who is blissfully unaware that we are at a crossroads in our lives.

This house, these people, and Jonny couldn't have been more welcoming. But can we really make a life here? It's not really the stuff of stories and definitely nothing like I imagined when I was growing up.

However, I always knew I didn't want the life my mom had. Don't ask me why, I just knew there was something better out there, so I smile and say with a yawn, "I'm sorry. I'm dead on my feet. I'm not good company."

Ashton says in a rush. "Of course. You've had a long traumatic day. If I thought you'd be ok with it, I'd offer to look after Hope for you, but I'm guessing you won't let her out of your sight after what those people did."

She looks so angry it makes me smile and I say gratefully, "Thank you. Maybe I'll take a rain check on that."

I say it more to make her feel better than mean it, because just the thought of Hope being out of my sight for a second has my heart frantically beating out of time.

Bonnie says firmly, "We should go. You have a man downstairs who is impatient to spend time with his family. We'll call on you tomorrow and take you shopping for supplies."

As they make to leave, I call out. "Thank you."

They turn and I blush a little as I say softly, "I don't deserve any of this, but thank you."

Ashton says fiercely, "You deserve every last thing and more. What you went through is monstrous and now you're here, you'll soon realize it's nowhere near as bad as it looks."

Bonnie nods. "That can all wait, though. Have a good evening, Faith."

I listen to them head downstairs and wander back into the nursery, loving how adorable everything is. I can't begin to imagine how much this all cost and I'm already fearful of receiving a huge check with no way to pay them back.

Hope stirs in my arms, and I set about changing and feeding her, loving the isolation now it's just the two of us.

For the first time in my life, I'm not afraid that my parents will heap more misery on my shoulders. It does feel safe here when it is probably anything but, and I should give it a chance.

"Hey."

I glance up and my heart flutters when I see Jonny standing in the doorway, delivering every fantasy I ever had.

"Hey." I smile and beckon him into the room.

He appears nervous and yet has a desperation in his eyes that I recognize and as he wanders over, he stares at Hope sleeping peacefully in her crib.

"She's perfect." He says almost to himself, and I love how besotted he is with her already.

"She is." I smile as I stare down at our little girl and then, as I raise my eyes, I see the love shining right back at me.

"I came back for you, Faith."

A simple statement that is loaded with regret and I say sadly, "I should never have run from you. I'm sorry."

He nods toward the open doorway, and I realize he must have many questions and so resigned to no sleep at all, I follow him outside. We must deal with this before we can move forward and what better time than the first day of the rest of our lives.

CHAPTER 30

JONNY

*H*ow can a man be happy and so anxious at the same time? Everything I ever wanted was in that room and yet it's as if it's hovering out of reach. What could be mine if I was a better man. A woman who loves me and a child so perfect she must have been crafted from the last shred of good in me.

I don't deserve them.

They are too good for me.

I am a cold-blooded killer.

A man who cusses, swears, and fucks whores in his spare time. A man running from the bitter words of his past and doing everything possible to prove them wrong but failing miserably.

I should never have gone back to Heaven, but I am so glad I did because I found a life worth fighting for. However, this fight may be one I can't win and so I need to test the water a little and see if there's a slight chance for Faith and for me.

I head into the kitchen and Faith follows nervously, babbling as she always does when she's nervous.

"This place is amazing, Jonny. I love what they've done

with it. Did you ever imagine places like this existed? What about Ashton and Bonnie? They are so cool, aren't they? They've made me so welcome. I really like them, you know…"

"Faith!" It comes out a little harder than I intended, and she jumps, her eyes wide and as she drags in that lower lip of hers and chews on it anxiously, it reminds me how she always had the ability to make me lose my mind.

"Faith." My voice is lower, desperate even, as I run my fingers through my hair and stare at her with a mixture of hope and fear.

"We need to talk."

Well, state the obvious. I sometimes hate my inability to form a meaningful sentence where she is concerned.

She nods and I point to the couch and hate that she sits straight-backed as if she's a passing visitor and not in her own home and I drop down before her on my knees, noting how her eyes widen and her anxious expression. I realize I'm a scary motherfucker. I intimidate most people, so I shrug out of my jacket that I really should get cleaned as a priority and face her as Jonny, the kid she told me she fell in love with.

"Faith." I don't appear to hold the power to move past her name, and I sigh and reach for her hands, taking each one in mine. She doesn't want to look me in the eye, that's obvious, so I say in a gentler tone, "Baby, look at me."

She peers nervously under her lashes and my heart crashes and burns as I am reminded of how innocent she is. What was I thinking bringing them here?

"I asked you to trust me."

My voice is husky and laced in desperation because I just can't fuck this up.

"I do." She whispers, and I smile ruefully.

"Then why did you run?"

Now it's out there I'm not sure I even want the answer to that and hate the tears that fill her eyes as she whispers, "Because I didn't want to ruin your life."

"My life. What do you mean?"

She chews on that god-damned lip again, causing the heat to flare inside me at the memory of how it tasted.

"I loved you so hard, Jonny."

I hate the past tense she uses, and she whispers, "You were everything to me. I loved you from the moment we knocked heads and you stared at me like nobody had ever stared at me before. You captured my heart in that moment and I would have done anything for you. I *did* everything for you."

"I don't understand."

I'm confused, and she grips my hands a little tighter and whispers, "You were my secret. The most treasured secret I never thought I'd hold. The local bad boy. A sinner in the eyes of the town. I couldn't admit to anyone how I felt about you because the brainwashed part of me was telling me that you were a devil sent by God to tempt me."

She rolls her eyes. "A lifetime of indoctrination counted for not a lot in the end because I discovered that love writes its own story and I fell for you hard."

"You are talking in the past tense, baby. I'm waiting for when it all changed."

I tense as I wait for her to break my heart all over again and am surprised when she drops my right hand and, reaching out, touches my face with a gentle pressure that is so good.

"I never stopped loving you, Jonny. How could I? You are my soul mate and if that means I have the soul of the devil, I will live with that."

I gaze into her eyes, having lost the power of speech as she whispers, "I ran to protect you, Jonny. To protect Hope and to protect myself. You understand how it works in

Heaven. If my parents learned I was pregnant, they would have the child beaten out of me."

I know she's right and say angrily, "That is precisely why you should have come to me. I would have taken care of you."

"You were leaving." She sounds so sad about that and says in a shaky voice. "You had a life outside Heaven. You had done the unthinkable and escaped. When you returned, I realized it wouldn't be for long and never thought for one second I deserved the right to ask you to take me with you."

I open my mouth the protest and she rests her finger against it and says sorrowfully, "I couldn't ask that of you, Jonny. To fight the town who would have shot you like a dog in the streets while I was made to watch. To be stoned like a witch for my sins and lose the life we had created from love. I ran to avoid all of that to protect us all. Our unborn baby and the life you had fought so hard to change. I ran to save us Jonny, and I thought I had succeeded."

Her voice trembles and I snarl, "Then how did they find you?"

Faith shakes her head. "Please, Jonny. Can we leave this because I am so tired, and Hope will wake soon for another feed?"

She smiles softly and whispers, "I'll tell you everything in the morning, but tonight ..." She hesitates.

"Please, will you just hold me?"

I make to pull her into my arms, and she hesitates before saying, "Not here. Um, well ...."

Her face flushes with embarrassment, which makes me smile. There she is, my innocent angel who just can't help wanting something she shouldn't.

"It will be my pleasure, darlin'." I whisper huskily and as I take her hand, I pull her to her feet and as we head up the stairs to bed, I already know I'm in for a torturous night.

CHAPTER 31

FAITH

Once again, I thank Ashton and Bonnie because everything I need is waiting for me. I shower and wash my hair, scrubbing every inch of the town I left behind from my body and wish it was as easy from my mind.

I drop the hated dress into the trash basket and pull on a beautiful satin slip to sleep in. Everything here is decadent and desirable, and so is the man waiting for me in the bedroom.

My heart beats furiously as I prepare to lie next to Jonny. It will be the first time because our time together was always snatched moments in hidden places. We were always conscious of being discovered, which brought a certain kind of urgency to our times together.

Tonight, is different. We have our space and for some reason I'm even more nervous because there is nowhere left to hide. I have dreamed of this moment ever since I met him and now the reality is scaring the shit out of me.

It feels so wrong to head into the softly lit room to offer myself to a man who is not my husband, but I realize it's just my upbringing coming back to bite me.

My heart quickens when I see him sitting on the edge of the bed, a white dressing gown covering his naked flesh, which is probably for my benefit.

He stares up at me as I head into the room, conscious of the soft fabric molding to my curves, and his eyes flash with desire that makes my heart skip a beat as he whispers softly, "You are so beautiful, Faith. You always were the prettiest girl in Heaven and now I know you are the most beautiful woman in the world."

I blush as he laughs softly and reaches out his hand, whispering, "Come here."

I don't know how my body moves I'm so nervous, but it has its own agenda and apparently can't reach him quickly enough.

As his hand runs around my waist, his eyes glitter as he whispers, "We can take it slow. Just sleep tonight if that's what you want. You don't have to do anything you don't want to."

Is he crazy? I have been dreaming of this moment my entire life, it seems, and I lower myself onto the bed beside him and whisper, "Is that what you want?"

I reach out and rest my hand on that insane chest that appears larger and even more desirable, and his tortured groan makes me smile as he says roughly, "Of course, it's not what I want."

His hand reaches out and cups my face and he says gruffly, "I want to love you, darlin'. To prove to you that I always have and remind you that I'm your man and always will be."

"Then do it." I say with a whispered excitement. "Show me how shameless I am and ruin my soul forever. I dare you."

I twist my lips into a wicked grin and love how his eyes flash with desire, drawing me deeper into the pit of hell.

I gasp, "I want to be a sinner with you, Jonny, because as it turns out, being an angel sucks."

His lips crash against mine and it's still there. That explosion that rocks my body every fucking time. It's a force of nature, a breaking storm and as we kiss like the lovers we were, it unleashes that part of me my parents feared.

Our tongues tangle and I love the rough scuff of his jaw grazing against my delicate skin, branding me as his.

He pushes me back onto the bed and I frantically tear his dressing gown away because the most important thing in my life right now is his skin sliding against mine.

My breath hitches when I see the strength of him. His well-defined muscles appear crafted from stone and the ink that decorates them should repel me with the images of skulls and daggers. However, one name above his heart has my pulse racing and as I trace the script, he holds my hand with his, flat against his heart and whispers huskily, "I gave you my heart, Faith."

The tears spring forward more with relief than anything, because his declaration of love is the sweetest gesture he could have made.

I stare at my name scripted across his heart and I say with a sob, "I love you, Jonny. I loved you from the day we knocked heads and you gazed into my eyes. It was that quick."

His eyes shine as he kisses me deeply, slowly and with increasing passion, and as his hand slides lower its met with even more heat. I am *burning* for him. Inside and out and it becomes the most important thing in my life to welcome him back where he belongs.

As I push forward with an urgency that even surprises me, he stops suddenly and whispers with a tortured groan, "I'm sorry, darlin', it's too much too soon."

"Don't you dare back out now, soldier."

He raises his eyes and I giggle. "Please, Jonny, we have waited too long already."

He doesn't say a fucking word and just grins like the devil he is as he pushes in slowly, savoring the moment as he claims what's his. He holds my chin in one hand and compels me to stare into his devilish eyes as he reminds me who is really in control of my body and mind.

It feels so good. It always did and as he swells inside me, filling me completely, I love every delicious second of it. Jonny is back where he belongs and the fact we're not married makes a sinful act even more special.

Jonny stares into my eyes with every thrust, every move and enjoys every gasp that spills from my lips. He can't tear his eyes away as he plays my body like a professional. It's as if he is claiming every inch of me and I stare right back at him with a sexy smile and all the love in my heart. I have waited for this moment, never really believing it was possible, and as the reality hits me, my orgasm crashes to meet it. We made it, we survived Heaven and as frightening as the future is right now, I wouldn't want to be anywhere else.

Jonny watches every second of my orgasm before his own crashes through my body, stripping it of any fight that may be lingering. I can't fight against this, fight against him. I already accept I couldn't run again if I tried. Jonny is my man, and I will always be his woman. I just hope he doesn't get bored with an innocent, naive woman from the town that America lost along the way.

"Shit." He growls against my neck as his cock throbs inside me and I say nervously, "What? Is there a problem?"

"I forgot to use a condom." He replies, sounding so upset I say gently, "It wouldn't be the first time."

I giggle against his shoulder and his low rumble of laughter makes me smile.

He pulls back and strokes my face lovingly and whispers,

"We're together now. A family. If that family increases, then I will be a happy man. There will be no mistakes in our life, Faith. Never any mistakes when we make such incredibly beautiful babies together."

My eyes are bright as his words calm my fears and I smile softly against his lips. "Do you mean that, Jonny? I mean, you may get bored with me and, well..."

I hate that I'm ruining the moment, but I can't help thinking of the women waiting in the wings just a block away.

He seems surprised and then the penny drops, and he grins as if he's enjoying every minute of my embarrassment.

"You think I'd prefer a whore over the only woman I have ever loved—will ever love?"

He shakes his head as if I've amused him and my face burns as I try to pull away. He's too strong though and grips me in a hard embrace and says forcefully, "I'm not going to pretend I haven't fucked anyone else, but yours was the only face I saw when I was doing it."

I'm stunned and strangely annoyed for the women and snap, "That's horrible. Those poor women."

He raises his eyes. "So, they're poor women now."

I grin, loving his playfulness and then his expression softens, and he whispers against my lips, "If I couldn't have you, I wanted the memory of you. I tried so hard to let go, but your face was all I could see. I chose women who looked like you, even though it felt as if I was betraying you."

He kisses me lightly on the lips before saying gruffly, "I was angry. You ran away from me, and I didn't understand why. I thought you regretted what happened between us and it killed me inside. For a long time, I was lost. I couldn't find my way back and fucking a lookalike was the only control I had left. I'm sorry if that shocks you and I'm sorry you will probably meet the women responsible, but I am not sorry that I loved you too damn much to let you leave my mind."

As Jonny kisses me with renewed passion, nothing else matters. All that does is in this house and any jealousy or pain I may experience for those lost years must be forgotten and replaced with excitement for our future. We are a family now and thank God, he brought us back together because the alternative is something I am sure will star forever in my nightmares.

CHAPTER 32

JONNY

*S*omehow, we found time to sleep in between fucking in every position and running to Hope when she woke between feeds. I wouldn't change a thing though because I have never felt as happy as I do tonight.

When the dawn breaks, Faith is out cold and as Hope cries from the other room, I resist waking her mother and head into the adorable nursery Ashton and Bonnie created for her.

I peer into the crib and my heart explodes with love for this child. I didn't know that unconditional love was a real thing because I certainly never experienced any of it myself. My own mother apparently hated me on sight. Probably due to the difficult birth that she threw in my face as a reason why I was evil.

'Even as a baby in the womb, you brought me pain.'

She would love to say as she struck me around the face for daring to play in the mud or speak out of turn.

There will be none of that for Hope. She can roll in the mud for all I care. I want her to be free, unapologetic where it counts, and not afraid to come to me with any of her problems. If she has any, you can bet I'll deal with them and as she glances up at me curiously with fresh tears sparkling in her lashes, I instinctively reach out and lift the small bundle of perfection into my arms.

She doesn't appear afraid of me like most people. She snuggles into my chest as if by some miracle I can feed her myself. It makes me smile and as I stare into her eyes, I smile softly and whisper, "I'm your daddy, Hope."

I head across to the window where the sun is putting on a fantastic show as it arrives for the blistering day ahead and I turn her to face the window and whisper, "This is the first day of the rest of our lives. The three of us. You, mommy and me. This is our home, and you have nothing to fear here."

I kiss her sweet little head and sound slightly husky with emotion. "You will have lots of friends and so much love you will buckle under the weight of it. A mommy who is already the best one in the world and a daddy who will love and protect you as every parent should. I can't promise you grandparents, but I can promise you a fierce family who will always love and protect you."

I can't resist dropping another light kiss on her soft little cheek and whisper, "You were born in Heaven but as it turns out, that place never really lived up to its name. Some call this place hell; I disagree because who wants to live in Heaven when Hell is way more fun?"

A soft chuckle alerts me that we're not alone and I turn and smile as Faith stands leaning against the door jamb, looking like an angel in the scrap of satin that I must thank Ashton and Bonnie for.

She appears sleepy but so darn beautiful I can't believe my luck and, as she heads across the room, she drapes her arm around my waist and gazes at Hope with a soft smile.

"Morning, baby." She whispers, dropping a light kiss on

her cheek, and then she turns to me and whispers huskily, "I swear I have never been so happy."

"Me too." Bending down, still with Hope against my naked chest, I kiss the woman I am besotted with in a long, lingering kiss.

When I pull away, I whisper, "This feels good."

"It does."

Hope stirs in my arms and Faith grins. "I probably should feed her. I usually give her the first one and then I'll make up some formula and you can do the next one, if you don't have to work, that is." She looks anxious and I shake my head. "No. I have the day to show you around and spend time with my family."

As she takes Hope from my arms, she says happily, "Thank you, Jonny."

"What for?" I can't tear my eyes from her as she settles in the big chair and places Hope to her breast.

"For coming back. For saving me and for rescuing Hope." She smiles down at our child and the expression of pure unadulterated love on her face has me spell-bound.

Then she lifts those beautiful eyes, and they sparkle with love aimed directly at my heart and she whispers, "For loving me enough to bring me here."

I head across the room and drop down before her and I swear everything I ever want is in this room.

"Will you marry me, Faith?"

The words come out fast because I can't waste any more time and the expression on her face tells me she wants this as much as I do.

"Of course, I'll marry you, Jonny. I love you."

The honest way she gazes at me, the innocent smile of an angel and the woman who has given me the greatest gift in the world, makes my own heart so full I could move mountains today.

"I love you too, darlin.'" I grin and peer down at my baby, who is sucking noisily and smile with so much love in my heart it may burst.

"I love you too, little one."

I gently stroke her head with one rough finger and conclude that this is my perfect moment. Where all the shit I have gone through matters and yet I wouldn't change a thing because ultimately everything that happened brought us to this point.

I hate to leave them, but I head downstairs to fix us coffee and as I familiarize myself with our gleaming new kitchen, I thank the Reapers from the bottom of my heart. There is no better life for my family than here. I already know that, but I'm still not certain that Faith will see it this way when she gets the tour later today.

With a deep sigh, I reach for the mugs and wonder if I should warn her of the depravation that happens in the huge bar at the end of the day. I'm almost fearful of what lies in wait because there are many men and women living at the Rubicon who enjoy what's on offer here a little too much.

The morning is spent being a family and I'm loving every minute of it.

When there's a knock on the door, I'm amazed to find we're not even dressed yet and Faith stares at me with horrified eyes. "Oh God, don't open the door, Jonny."

I love her so much in that silk barely there nightdress, I wish she could wear it all day, but I just cock my head to the stairs with a resigned, "I'll answer it. You head upstairs and change."

She smiles gratefully and then with a check on Hope who is sleeping, yet again, in her stroller, she heads upstairs like a rocket as I head toward the door.

Ashton and Bonnie stand outside with knowing grins on their faces when they see me bare-chested and wearing nothing but my Calvin's.

"Heavy night?" Bonnie grins and Ashton giggles as I run my fingers through my hair and stand to one side.

"I don't know what you mean." I wink as they pass and Ashton says in her soft drawl, "We thought Faith may appreciate a tour. It's such a lovely day, and she could use some fresh air."

"Sure, she's just getting ready. She won't be long."

Bonnie glances at her watch. "It's midday." Her eyes are wide, and Ashton says quickly, "When I had Caspian, sometimes I never dressed all day. Babies take up so much of your time and when they sleep you make use of that time to, well, to get organized."

She blushes a little and Bonnie laughs out loud. "Then don't tell Snake, or I'll remain childless forever."

We glance up as Faith heads down the stairs in a gorgeous cornflower blue sundress, and I don't believe I have ever seen her look as pretty. Her hair is secured in a band behind her neck and her eyes are bright with happiness. I even forget we have visitors and can't resist heading her way and pulling her into my arms, kissing her softly as I grip on to the ponytail, vowing to make use of this later.

She pushes me away, her face burning, and the girls laugh when she whispers, "Fuck, Jonny, we have visitors."

She nods toward my growing interest in her and, laughing, I say over my shoulder, "I'll leave you girls to it. Don't keep her too long."

Their laughter follows me upstairs and when I reach the top, I hear Faith say breathlessly, "I'm so sorry, what must you think of us?"

It makes me smile at my innocent angel and then grin as Bonnie says loudly, "Man, that was nothing. If we have visitors, they may get more than just an eyeful when Snake is horny."

Ashton giggles and I can only imagine the expression on Faith's face because she will not be used to this. She has probably never been around women like Bonnie, and I thank Ryder for sending his wife with her because Ashton is the sweetest angel shining at the top of the Rubicon tree, keeping the air pure and somehow managing to deal with the biggest bastard in here. If anyone can educate my old lady, she is the perfect one for the job.

CHAPTER 33

FAITH

*I*t feels so good walking around this place in the bright sunlight with two women who couldn't have been more welcoming. As I push the stroller with Hope sleeping like an angel, Ashton says wistfully, "Man, this makes me broody."

Bonnie nods. "I'm always broody these days."

"What's stopping you then?" Ashton says curiously and I note the resignation on Bonnie's face.

"Snake wants kids like tomorrow, but I've only just qualified as an interior designer and want to establish my business first. I told him next year would be convenient."

Ashton catches my eye and shakes her head.

"I'm sure Faith will tell you it was most *inconvenient* when she had her baby, but I'm guessing she wouldn't change a thing. Tell her, Faith."

I nod, gazing at my perfect daughter and say happily, "When I found out I was pregnant, I was horrified. Terrified even because I was so uneducated, I didn't realize it would be that easy."

We reach an area facing the mountains, where there are comfortable seats set around a pretty garden.

Ashton takes one of the seats and the Bonnie the other and as we settle down, I find myself unburdening a little.

"It must have been terrifying." Ashton smiles with concern and I nod, thinking back on my darkest days.

"Jonny was due to take up a new position. We both knew that day was coming and talked about it at length. He told me he would arrange for me to join him, and even the thought of that terrified me."

I say with a sigh. "Life in Heaven was controlled, hard and emotionless. We were brought up to fear God and respect the bible. We were indoctrinated and just the fact I had kissed Jonny was a sin in the townsfolk's eyes, let alone what we did in secret."

Bonnie shakes her head with disgust. "Fucking weird shit."

It makes me laugh and I nod. "You could say that. Then Jonny left. He had a new job, and I used to hear the whispers calling him evil, a devil in disguise and a child who had strayed from the path into darkness."

"Fuck me."

Bonnie whistles and Ashton says sadly. "No wonder you were anxious."

"That's putting it mildly."

I say sadly, "Jonny told me he would set things up and then come and get me. I really believed he would, and I planned for our future. I couldn't wait to leave Heaven and experience first-hand what he spoke about. He made it sound so exciting I could put up with life in Heaven while he was gone, knowing I had a way out."

"What happened next?"

Bonnie's eyes are wide, and she completely ignores Ashton's warning stare and I say in a low voice, "I became sick. At least I thought I'd caught something and when I vomited outside the general store one day, the owner, Martha, was on hand. She helped clean me up and I'll never forget the fear in her eyes when she asked if I may be pregnant. I'd never even considered it and dismissed the weight I put on as something that happened naturally."

"You weren't wrong." Bonnie adds and Ashton says irritably, "Let her finish."

They lean forward and I say sadly, "She produced a test. God knows I didn't even realize things like that existed, and it didn't take long to confirm I was pregnant."

I shiver involuntarily and whisper, "It was a disaster. I had committed the ultimate sin in Heaven. I was no longer a virgin and had slept with the devil."

"What the..." Bonnie makes to speak and Ashton places her hand on her arm and says hastily, "You poor thing. It must have been awful."

I nod. "I was in shock and thank God Martha was the one who discovered my sin, and I will be eternally grateful to her for that."

"I'm sorry..." Bonnie says in a hard voice and holds up her hand as Ashton makes to speak.

"You do know it wasn't a sin, don't you because quite frankly, if you say yes, I'm liable to beat the shit out of you myself?"

It makes me laugh as Ashton says, "Bonnie!" The horror in her voice making me smile.

"It's fine." I smile at the two women who couldn't be nicer. "I know that now, but at the time I never knew differently."

"So, what happened next?" Ashton says softly and I turn to look at Hope, still sleeping peacefully, unaware of her tough beginning.

"Martha was a saint. She helped me leave town."

"Wow! I'm loving Martha already." Bonnie adds, and I

nod. "She was amazing. In fact, her husband is a huge fan of Jonny's and helped us escape a second time. We owe them so much."

"So, what happened next?"

Bonnie leans forward and I smile, loving how unapologetic she is.

"Only two people knew of my situation. Martha and my best friend Purity."

"Fuck me." Bonnie interrupts. "Are you people for real? What's with the saintly names?"

Ashton groans and puts her head in her hands. "I'm so sorry, Faith. Bonnie comes with no filter attached."

It makes me laugh. "It is a little strange. I'll admit that. Anyway, Purity helped me by finding stuff for me to take on my journey. She helped hide it away and acted as my alibi to give me time to escape."

"She sounds like a good friend." Ashton smiles gently.

"She is." I nod, my heart softening when I think of her, and I carry on with my story.

"Martha hid me in the back of Mr. Gaston's truck. He left town once a week to get supplies in the nearest large town. Martha had arranged for shelter at a women's refuge in a place called Diamond Springs on Purity's recommendation. I had never heard of it, but she assured me they would help me. I was so excited and yet scared at the same time. I had never been past the county line before, and now I was running away. If they found me, my life wouldn't be worth living, but if I stayed, I may have ended up under a barrage of rocks thrown my way."

Bonnie holds up her hand and says angrily, "Wait, what? Are you freaking kidding me? Rock slinging. What's that all about? And I really hope you're talking metaphorically."

"Unfortunately, no."

I shake my head. "The fact I was carrying the spawn of the

devil in their eyes meant I had committed two unforgiveable sins. I was no longer innocent and would be punished by stoning. They would kill my unborn child as punishment for my sins and then I would be labeled as the town whore and a sinner."

"Fuck me." Ashton says, which makes me giggle because unlike Bonnie, she doesn't appear the type to curse.

"Respect for Martha. I love that woman," Bonnie says in a voice laced with anger and I nod, smiling as I think back on the woman who saved my life along with Hope's.

"So, what happened when you got to Diamond Springs?"

Ashton presses on and I say sadly, "I was so afraid. I had never seen a town like that in my life. I was alone and carrying a huge burden in my eyes at the time. They took me in at the refuge and even gave me a job waiting tables at the nearby diner. I learned a lot there in the months I was alone and best of all, I discovered nobody judged me. They were friendly, kind, and helpful and I even began to believe I was free."

"What about Jonny? He would have made everything okay. Why didn't you contact him?"

"Because I didn't want to ruin his life."

"I don't understand?" Ashton's eyes are wide, and I sigh heavily. "Jonny was just starting out like me. He had a job to do, and I didn't want him to carry the burden of having two other lives to worry about. If word got out about what he did to me, his own family would have shot him dead as soon as he entered their home."

"You're kidding me." Bonnie says in horror, and I sigh heavily. "Life in Heaven was basic, and we lived by the teachings of the bible, at least the ones the reverend wanted us to know. If the town learned of what we did, we would be dead because of it."

"So, why did you go back?" Ashton says in confusion, and

I shudder. "I had no choice. When I had Hope, I woke up to find my parents by the side of my bed with Hope already on her way back to Heaven."

"But how? They couldn't take your baby without your consent," Ashton says in disgust.

I shake my head. "They had papers saying I was unfit to care for a child and as they were my legal guardians, the hospital was powerless. They weren't alone either. Reverend Peters accompanied them and the entire journey home, he prayed for my soul as I cried for my child."

"This is like something out of a movie." Bonnie says sadly and I nod. "It was reality for us. When we returned, they locked me in my room with Hope for weeks while they tried to figure a way out of the mess I created. Gradually, news of my sin reached the town and one day they made me kneel at the altar and repent my sins in front of the entire town. My punishment was to raise my bastard child, as they called her, and work scrubbing the church. To endure daily bible studies to learn what was expected of me, while they figured out the rest of my life."

"So, how did Jonny rescue you?" Bonnie says quickly and I smile. "When the reverend's wife died, they told me I would replace her. He would beat the devil from my soul, and I would repent my sin under his watchful control."

"Man." Bonnie shakes her head. "The sick bastard."

I shiver at the memory of that time and say with a smile. "Then Jonny returned for a visit."

"You must have been relieved to see him." Ashton smiles warmly and I nod, my eyes softening at the memory.

"Yes, and once again, my friends helped me escape."

"Purity and Martha." Ashton grins and I nod, forever grateful to the only people in that town I care about.

"Mr. Gaston and Purity helped Jonny by telling him

where I was, but they left me to break the news of our daughter."

We hear voices approaching and Ashton says with a groan. "Thank God it all worked out in the end."

I look up and wonder about that statement when I see two women deep in conversation, dressed in the tightest shorts that barely cover their ass and tight t-shirts that definitely don't cover their chests.

They stop and stare at us and say with a friendly nod, "Ladies."

They stare at me with a curiosity that doesn't go unnoticed, and Bonnie says loudly, "Hey guys, come and meet Sinner's old lady and his adorable daughter, Hope."

As they turn to look at me, I register the surprise on their faces and one of them shakes her head and says loudly, "Oh fuck. Another one bites the dust."

Her friend nudges her and they grin as they head my way and I prepare to meet a couple of so-called whores, not really knowing what to expect.

CHAPTER 34

JONNY

I'm not sure this is such a good idea but recognize it needs to be done sooner rather than later.

When Faith told me she wanted to head to the bar tonight, the anxiety hit me hard.

Now she looks a million dollars as she heads down the stairs, a vision in tight jeans and a pretty white top. Her hair styled in bouncy waves and her make-up natural but designed to give her the confidence she will need.

"They did a good job, huh?" She spins around as she references the two whore's work who couldn't wait to get their hands on her.

I was worried when she struck up a friendship with Beth and Peony, although I needn't have worried. They are the sweetest girls, who are waiting out their time here until they decide what happens next. They call themselves whores, the Reapers call them fallen angels. Women we've rescued from unhappy beginnings who are given a place to stay while they figure out their next move.

Some move on quickly, others hang around, happy in the

life we provide. If I was worried that Faith would find that difficult to cope with, I couldn't be more wrong.

It's been three days since we arrived here, and I have loved every minute of it. We are a family, and I am falling harder for both of my girls every single minute that ticks by.

I love watching a movie with Hope resting her sweet soft head on my naked chest, as Faith sits beside me, her fingers tangled in mine as we enjoy quiet time away from the madness, content to be together.

Then when Hope sleeps, we make up for lost time and there is no inch of my woman I haven't explored several times over. Sex comes so naturally to me and Faith. As if we knew the lines before we even read the script. She is everything I ever wanted and never deserved, and we have spoken at length about our demons, putting them to rest so they don't continue with us on our journey.

However, tonight there is one fucking big demon who needs to be slain and a loud knock on the door tells me that moment has arrived.

I head to open it and find Lou, Brewers' wife, waiting on the porch and she smiles. "Hey, Sinner. It's judgment day."

She laughs softly because she's seen this all before. A woman's first time in the compound bar is make or break for the Reaper who brought her there. Not many understand our ways and it's a hard ask, but I'm hoping Faith will see beyond the lecherous Reapers and accept it for what it is. A place to relax and recover from the horrors of the day. To let off steam and mix with like-minded people who have the best hearts and intentions wrapped in sin.

As we prepare to head outside, Lou winks at Faith. "Hey, honey. Don't you worry about a thing. I know where you are if Hope wants her mommy. Although she's such an angel, I doubt I'll hear a cry from her all night."

It amuses me how Brewer's old lady has taken Faith under

her wing. They were introduced the day we arrived and have struck up an easy friendship. Lou is older than most of the Reapers old ladies and she tells a good story. She also knows exactly how to deal with this life and is respected by everyone and adored by them all.

"Thanks, Lou." Faith smiles and I immediately contemplate sending Lou home. Faith looks so gorgeous tonight I'd rather just spend the night buried deep inside her. However, even I realize she needs to mix and understand this life, so with an irritable sigh, I say wearily, "Let's get this shit over with."

Lou raises her eyes as Faith looks worried and smiles warmly. "Keep an open mind, honey. You've met some of the Reapers already and some of the girls. The only shocking thing is when the two halves meet, it causes a few explosions."

She winks as I say with a tortured groan. "If Faith hates me after tonight, I'm holding you responsible, Lou."

"I'm just telling it how it is. You'll be fine."

Lou winks at Faith, who looks a little worried, and I hold out my hand and say gruffly, "Come on, darlin'. It's time to face your fears."

"More like yours, Sinner." Lou laughs as she settles on the couch and opens her book. "Don't be back too soon. I'm grateful for some 'me' time away from the shit waiting at home."

Faith looks concerned and so I add, "Lou's son Jack can be a bit of a handful, as I'm sure you've already discovered."

Faith grins. "He was fighting with Cassie earlier, and they didn't see Ryder coming."

"What happened?" I grin because Cassie is a lot like her father, and he encourages her more than he reprimands her.

"He made them fight it out supervised." Faith shakes her head as Lou laughs.

"Usual story. They beat the shit out of each other and ended the fight as the best friends they always were."

"Ryder's a bad ass. I couldn't watch a guy beating the shit out of Hope. If I notice a guy even look her way, he won't look again."

Lou catches Faith's eye and grins. "Good luck with that, soldier."

She grins. "Now off you go. I'm at a very important chapter in my book and I'm impatient to get into it."

As we leave her to it, I lace my fingers with Faith's and love how we walk like any normal couple out for an evening stroll. The crickets are singing loudly in the bushes and the moon is beating down on us, surrounded by the brightest stars.

Faith looks up at them and sighs. "Do you remember that night I snuck out to meet you?"

"I will never forget it."

She references the night she gave her virginity to me, and I will *never* forget that.

"It was so special lying on that blanket under the stars. I really believed nothing could ever tear us apart."

"It didn't." I remind her and she stops suddenly and says earnestly, "I'm sorry I ran, Jonny. I was scared for you—for us. If they discovered it was you, they would shoot you dead, and I had to protect you both."

I remember the pain that I carried with me for close on two years and it's as if I let her down when she needed me most.

Tipping her face to mine, I whisper huskily, "I let you down, baby. You should have known I would never allow anything to happen to either of us."

"How? We may have been close, Jonny, but we had so few

moments together we were virtually strangers. Most of our time was spent doing other things rather than talking— remember?"

She smiles shyly, and it's as if a star has fallen from the sky and I am holding the brightest one in my arms. I kiss her deeply under the same stars we found one another and then, pulling back, I say huskily, "My biggest regret is that I stopped searching. I believed Purity when she told me you didn't want me. That you had run away to escape me."

"Don't blame Purity, Jonny. She tried so hard to change my mind. She called me stupid and cruel and didn't want any part of it because you were the best thing that had ever happened to me, and I was a fool to turn my back on that."

This is news to me, and I say incredulously, "Then why didn't you listen?"

"Because I let my fear control me. I had lived with it so long it was all I knew. But not now. Not now my eyes have opened, and I've seen the whole picture. I feel like a fool, and she was right to call me out on it."

"She was a good friend." I say, remembering her loyalty to Faith by keeping it all to her herself, even as it turns out, against her own better judgment.

"Do you think she'll be ok, Jonny? I'm worried about her."

I nod, because the same thought has crossed my mind already because a woman like Purity isn't equipped to deal with the real world and I say with determination. "I'll see what I can find out."

Her soft smile has me reaching for those tempting lips all over again and as we kiss like the lovers were are, I wish we could recreate the most special night of my life, right now instead of heading to a place that may change her mind entirely.

CHAPTER 35

FAITH

I'm not sure why I'm so anxious, but as we reach the steel compound that I have avoided up until now, the nerves are almost consuming me. Ashton and Bonnie offered to show me the bar area when it was quiet, but even then, I didn't want to go there. I suppose it's because everything is going so well with Jonny. I didn't want anything to mess with that and yet as we near the huge structure I have a hard word with myself, because whatever Jonny did before I came here is his business and definitely not any of mine.

He seems nervous too and I feel bad about that. It's my job to reassure him, so I say softly, "It will be fine. I'm a big girl now. I can cope with what's inside."

"I know."

He grins. "You are the strongest woman I have ever met because you survived Heaven."

We share a smile, both of us the only people here who can ever really understand what we went through, and as I take his hand, I squeeze it with a reassurance I really want him to believe. With a deep breath, he pushes open the door and the noise alone confuses me because it's so incredibly loud. Heavy Rock makes the floor thump, above which are loud voices and a lot of laughter. I want to hide behind Jonny so badly but stand my ground and stare in surprise at a place that makes me smile. It appears that everyone is having a really good time as I stare at men and women who obviously don't give a shit about anything other than having the most fun they can.

A huge bar runs the length of the room in front of which are couches set around tables. There are bar stools holding large, tattooed bikers and many women laughing with them as they chat among themselves. At one end are a couple of pool tables and I notice one woman bend over it as she tries to sink her shot, a biker helping her as he rests his large hand on her ass.

Many of the guys look our way and call out to Jonny who returns their greetings with an easy acceptance of the situation, and I don't miss the curious glances of both bikers and whores as I stand beside him, feeling as if I shouldn't be here.

Jonny grips my hand hard and guides me through the crowd, and I even note a few familiar faces as they say hi. I register Blade sitting with his arm around a petite blonde, who is giggling at something he's whispering in her ear and as he looks up, he flashes a broad welcoming smile.

"Hey, darlin', how is that cute little baby of mine?"

The girl stares at me in shock and Jonny growls, "In your dreams, Blade."

He merely bursts out laughing and winks at me, and then I notice Bonnie waving madly from the bar as she stands beside the man they call Snake. Her old man, as she calls him.

I smile because I will be eternally grateful to him and Flash for their help when they waited with me outside the church. He is a force of nature as he towers above her, his muscles flexing against the striking tattoo of a king cobra snake that winds up his arm and finishes at his neck. He is possibly even scarier than Blade and I swallow hard as his dark eyes glitter as we approach and now I know why Bonnie needs to be tough because her man appears to be the toughest guy I have ever met.

"Come and sit with us guys. Ryder and Ashton won't be long, and we want to welcome Faith the Reaper way." Bonnie says with excitement.

Now I'm nervous, especially when Jonny grins wickedly and I whisper, "I don't like the sound of that."

He slides his arm around my waist and whispers, "I've got your back, baby."

Now I'm even more afraid and yet don't have a chance to think about it when the jeers get even louder and it's as if a celebrity has entered the room. A chorus of greetings makes me turn to see Ryder and Ashton enter the bar. Once again, I do a double take because I have never seen a more perfect couple in my life.

It's as if Ryder King, their president, is untouchable. He surrounds himself with an air of authority that warns everyone away. The protective way he is holding Ashton's hand, and the gentle looks he saves only for her, warms my soul. I have never experienced raw loving like I have here. They are a family, an amazing one because in all my life, I have never witnessed a scene like this.

In Heaven, the townsfolk are polite and reserved, too afraid to speak out of turn and be ostracized from society. It's almost as if they live their life on automation. Not living, just existing, and if my parents could see me now, they would pray for my soul for the whole of eternity.

I watch as Ashton and Ryder work the room and it appears as if everyone wants a piece of them. They stop and chat and I note how pretty Ashton is and that Ryder's arm never leaves her shoulder. If ever I saw a power couple, they are the best walking advert for one and it must be at least ten minutes later that they reach us.

"I need a fucking drink." Ryder moans and almost immediately a beer is pushed his way from the pretty girl behind the bar. She slides a wine glass in Ashton's direction and Ashton replies with a sweet, "You're an angel, Sunday."

She turns to me and says in her soft drawl. "Have you met Sunday, Faith?"

I shake my head shyly and she draws me over to meet the woman who appears a little older than me. She has wide green eyes and lavender hair and her figure is tall and slim. I should hate her with a passion but the soft smile she directs my way disarms me in a heartbeat. "You must be Faith. Sinner has told me all about you. Welcome to the Reapers, honey."

I stiffen at the reference to Jonny and wonder if she's one of the women he fucked. Jonny leans down and whispers in my ear, "I know what you're thinking, and we are just friends. For your information, more like brother and sister, and she's been a good listener."

He points to a guy leaning against the end of the bar and as I turn, my heart skips a beat at the huge guy glowering into his beer.

"She hooks up with Razor because she's the only one he can tolerate around him." Sinner explains in a low voice.

My heart beats faster because that man looks like a brute. He wears anger like a shield, and I stare as he taps the bar with heavily ringed fingers, his muscles straining against the ink decorating his arms, his t-shirt doing a miserable job of trying to cover his huge chest. His hair is dusting his shoulders, much like Blades and now I think of it, he does look quite similar, and Sunday catches my expression and smiles impishly. Then she leans forward and whispers, "They're brothers."

"Blade?"

I say in surprise, and she nods. "Twins actually, but Blade got all the humor and Razor was left with the anger."

As if he can sense us watching him, he turns and my breath hitches at the dark flashing eyes that could strike a man dead on the spot through fear and Sunday sighs.

"I'll check on what he wants. Great to meet you, Faith. Maybe we could grab a coffee sometime. I heard you have the cutest baby in the world, and I adore babies."

She grins and heads off down the bar, and I watch with interest as she stops in front of Razor and leans forward. He whispers something in her ear, and she reaches out and traces a light trail down his face and I stare in fascination as he extends a huge arm and pulls her closer, devouring her lips as if he is a starving man.

Bonnie says with a grin. "That man is stubborn as fuck and won't admit he has caught feelings for Sunday."

Ashton nods. "He pushes her away one minute and then can't leave her alone the next."

"Is she…" I can't even say the word and Bonnie grins wickedly. "A whore?"

I nod, feeling as if I'm talking out of turn and Bonnie shakes her head. "Technically, yes, but as we told you, these girls write their own agenda. Razor has made it crystal clear that Sunday is his exclusive property, and she is so sweet she wouldn't want to upset him."

"So, they are exclusive." I probe and Bonnie sighs.

"Not officially. You see, Sunday has options and could leave any time, and it's tearing Razor up inside. He won't hold her back but won't go with her, and that's where they are. Stalemate."

I notice Jonny laughing with Ryder and Snake and as he catches my eye, he winks, which makes my heart flutter because Jonny always did have the ability to shatter any principles I had because he is so damn sexy, my heart physically aches for him.

Once again, I glance down at the end of the bar and note the couple deep in conversation that is interrupted when another man joins them. I swear every man here is eye candy of the sweetest kind and when I see how cute they are with the women, it drives any fear I had away. Jonny was right. I do love it here and I'm strangely more at home than I ever was in Heaven.

By the end of the evening, any doubts I had have been firmly dealt with and I am looking forward to a lifetime filled with laughter and happiness. My mind has been settled and as we head home, I say impulsively, "Jonny."

"What, angel?"

"Thank you for bringing us here."

"Thank you for agreeing to it."

He smiles and in the light of the moon, he appears so desirable, so sexy and so dangerous and I don't know if a little of the debauchery in the bar has rubbed off on me, but I say impulsively, "Our back yard."

"What of it?"

"Can anybody see in?"

"I don't think so. Why?"

"I kind of want to revisit a memory."

His eyes sparkle in the dusky light as he understands my request, and without saying a word, he takes my hand and leads me home.

CHAPTER 36

JONNY

I didn't think life could get any better than this, but it has. In one sentence Faith has told me everything I needed to hear and while she chats shit with Lou, I head outside and make the preparations.

Then I sit and wait while she checks on Hope and when the back door opens, I see an angel framed in the doorway.

Faith is dressed in nothing but a warm blanket and my eyes devour her. She has never looked so beautiful as the dusky light catches the highlights in her hair. Her eyes are sultry and her smile sexy as she heads toward me where I'm sitting on the blanket.

"You came." I say in a low husky voice, and she nods.

"I had to wait until they were sleeping and snuck out through my bedroom window."

"I'm glad you made it." I say with a small smile and hold out my hand, so she drops beside me, her face flushed and her breathing shallow.

"We shouldn't be doing this." She says fearfully as she looks around her and I wrap her in my arms and whisper, "I won't tell if you won't."

As we kiss under the light of the moon, my feelings notch up another gear. She is so trusting; such an innocent angel and she is like a breath of fresh air in my toxic world.

As we kiss, the silence serenades us and only the sound of our lips touching, and her small moans disturb the night air. I ease the blanket from her shoulders and gently kiss a path down to her breasts and love how she gasps as I take one of her nipples into my mouth.

She throws her head back and I lick a path up to her slender neck and savor the taste of innocence. She feels so good as she shivers against me and soon the irritation of my clothes becomes too much to bear.

She helps me pull off my t-shirt and as I loosen my belt, I whisper, "Are you sure you want this, angel?"

"Yes, Jonny." Her voice is high and slightly breathless as she whispers, "More than anything."

I am driven crazy with lust and in this moment, really feel as if I'm invincible. Nothing can ever tear us apart. We will be together forever, us against the world, and as soon as her soft breasts brush against my bare chest, it unleashes the beast inside me, and I pounce.

I push her back on the blanket and devour every inch of her. Licking, sucking and loving every sound that comes from deep inside her. She is a freshly opened flower, the dew of a summer's morning and the fresh scent of Spring when the flowers start to bloom. She is my everything and I want the whole of her and as I nestle my face between her thighs, her shocked gasp makes me smile. I suck her sodden clit into my mouth, loving how she tastes like honey and the most forbidden treat, and as I coax her orgasm from deep inside her, I feel invincible.

My own throbbing cock is begging for something I'm not convinced I deserve and as she rides her last wave, she whispers, "Make me your woman, Jonny."

I hesitate for a second and she pleads, "I mean it. I want this. I want *you*. It must be you."

I swear my balls are about to explode as I move up her body until my swollen crown hovers uncertainly against her pussy and she pleads, "It's not enough. I want more. I want the whole of you."

This time as I thrust inside, her moan is almost feral and as she wraps those legs around me, I push in hard and fast. On and on, as if I have something to prove and I suppose I do. To her, to me and to the fucking town we were brought up in because this is not the action of a sinner, it's one of love. Love for the woman who is trusting me to do the right thing and just in time I remember and make to pull out.

"What?" she says in a worried voice, and I groan, "Condom."

Her soft giggle makes me smile as she says softly, "We live at the Rubicon, honey. I think we're already past the point of no return."

As I smooth her hair back with my hand and stare lovingly into her eyes, I whisper, "But what if…"

She silences me with a kiss and whispers, "A condom failed the first time. Let's give this one a helping hand."

"You mean …"

I love that I'm deep inside my woman when she says breathlessly, "We're revisiting a memory, Jonny. This is the perfect time to allow history to repeat itself and hope that we are as lucky the second time around."

It's all the reassurance I need, and I move inside her, staring into her gorgeous face the entire time, loving how she bites down on that swollen bottom lip and her eyes flash with lust as I fill her completely.

Like the last time, I come just as hard, and as Faith's soft cry fills the night air, I bask in her orgasm as she clenches my cock and know this will never get old.

For the longest time I lie clutching her tightly against me, buried deep inside, loving the fact we are as close as any couple can be. However, *unlike* the first time, as we lie entwined in one another's arms gazing up at the stars, we have no home to run back to. No escape to make before anyone discovers us and nobody to judge us anymore. We are free and this time I won't be watching her disappear over the horizon because somehow Faith made it back to me and there is no man or woman alive who can get in the way of that.

EPILOGUE

JONNY

THREE WEEKS LATER

I never dared hope life would get much better, but it has. I am happier than I have ever been in my life and all because of the two ladies who I come home to every night.

Business is slow, which suits me just fine, and Ryder proves why he so respected when he leaves me as part of the crew who remain at the compound when they head off on the few jobs that come in.

Faith is happy, Hope is happy, and I am ecstatic because I have everything I need. I have no urge to see my parents ever again and except for her mom, Faith is happy to leave her own as a bad memory. I know she has written to her mom, but so far nothing has been sent by return.

Word is that Heaven has been inundated with cops, social workers and do-gooders who are intent on dragging it into line with the rest of the country. Satellite television, even a mayor and their very own sheriff's department. Heaven will no longer get away with making their own rules, and I am more than happy about that.

Many people view us as dirty bikers when we ride into town. We play on the image but we are so much more than that. We clean up the government's shit with no questions asked but our missions never make the news. We work undercover and take out the bad guys, leaving the good people of America to sleep safely in their beds.

What happened back in Heaven was inevitable and it was the sweetest revenge for a childhood of abuse and vicious attacks.

When I am called to Ryder's office, I immediately sense something is wrong and his grave expression tells me I'm not going to like it.

Snake is sitting in the corner as usual and Brewer is on the couch. All the men are on alert, and I'm surprised to see Rebel sitting beside Brewer.

"What's up?" I kick out a chair and sit astride it as Ryder nods to Rebel.

"Tell him what you know."

Rebel fixes me with a worried frown.

"Faith's friend, Purity."

The blood drains from my face as I fear the worst.

"I gave her my phone." He continues. "I heard nothing, so Brewer traced the signal. It's not good man."

"Where is she?" I growl, fearful for the strong, brave woman who helped us with no regard for her own safety.

Rebel glances at Ryder and then says with a sigh, "Her current location is the Vieri mansion in Chicago."

"Fuck." I run my fingers through my hair and Ryder says in his deep drawl, "Rebel called the number, and she picked up."

"Thank God for that, at least."

I say with considerable relief and Snake snaps, "Told him she was handling it and not to worry, whatever that means."

I shake my head. "So, what's the problem?"

Ryder stares at me with a deep frown. "The Vieri mansion is the home of the supreme Dark Lord. Don Vieri. Purity may not realize this, but she's in danger."

"You think they carry out rituals like the Matassos?" I say incredulously. "We discovered that stopped years ago regarding the Dark Lords themselves."

"It's not that." Ryder sighs and spins his computer around to a headline on the local news.

Chicago's resident billionaire Killian Vieri is about to break the hearts of every single female in America. Today he announced his engagement to an unknown woman. They were snapped leaving The Vieri mansion as they enjoyed a night on the family yacht. Little is known of the woman who has captured his heart as Killian is known to take his privacy very seriously, but it is rumored the wedding will take place in Italy next month on the private island the family own.

"What the fuck?" I stare at the monitor in shock when I see the man himself holding Purity's hand and Ryder says with a worried frown. "Something doesn't feel right about this. Any guesses?"

None of us speak and he sighs heavily.

"I really hoped this shit was done when Carlos Matasso met his executioner. Now this Dark Lord's shit has come back to haunt us with an even more formidable adversary."

"It may be nothing." They stare at me in surprise, and I shrug. "They may have fallen in love. Purity is a rare beauty with the personality of an assassin. I'm pretty certain any man would be intoxicated by that, even a man as hardened as Killian Vieri."

"I doubt it." Ryder says wearily. "There is something he wants, and he's using her to get it. We need to re-open the file and start searching before it's too late for the innocent woman who has walked from one nightmare into another."

Snake grins and his eyes flash as Brewer laughs softly. Rebel looks worried and I share his concern.

Ryder, however, just fixes us all with a dark glower and says with a sigh. "Here we fucking go again."

* * *

Do you want to know what happened when Jonny first met Faith.
Carry on Reading

Catch up with Purity in

my new series
The Dark Lords

If you enjoyed this Reaper Romance, you will be happy to discover there are many more.
Catch up with Ryder in Daddy's Girls
Snake in Dirty Hero

They are not alone either. This is my world of strong heroes and sassy heroines. An MC Club with a difference and many tales of honor and courage.

Check them out at stellaandrews.com

Thank you for reading this story.
If you have enjoyed the fantasy world of this novel, please would you be so kind as to leave a review on Amazon?

Join my closed Facebook Group

Stella's Sexy Readers

Follow me on Instagram

Carry on reading for more Reaper Romances, Mafia Romance & more.
Remember to grab your free book by visiting stellaandrews.com.

. . .

ALSO BY STELLA ANDREWS

Twisted Reapers

Rebel

Dirty Hero (Snake & Bonnie)
Daddy's Girls (Ryder & Ashton)
Twisted (Sam & Kitty)
The Billion Dollar baby (Tyler & Sydney)
Bodyguard (Jet & Lucy)
Flash (Flash & Jennifer)
Country Girl (Tyson & Sunny)
Brutal Sinner (Jonny & Faith)

The Romanos
The Throne of Pain (Lucian & Riley)
The Throne of Hate (Dante & Isabella)
The Throne of Fear (Romeo & Ivy)
Lorenzo's story is in Broken Beauty

Beauty Series
*Breaking Beauty (Sebastian & Angel) **
Owning Beauty (Tobias & Anastasia)
*Broken Beauty (Maverick & Sophia) **
Completing Beauty – The series

Five Kings
Catch a King (Sawyer & Millie) *

<u>Slade</u>

Steal a King

Break a King

Destroy a King

Marry a King

Baron

Club Mafia

Club Mafia – The Contract

Club Mafia – The Boss

Club Mafia – The Angel

Club Mafia – The Savage

Club Mafia - The Beast

Club Mafia – The Demon

Ortega Mafia

The Enforcer

The Consigliere

The Don

The Dark lords

Pure Evil

A Shade of Evil

Pretty Evil

Born Evil

Standalone

The Highest Bidder (Logan & Samantha)

Rocked (Jax & Emily)

Brutally British

Fiercely British

Deck the Boss

Reasons to sign up to my mailing list.

•A reminder that you can read my books FREE with Kindle Unlimited.

•Receive a weekly newsletter so you don't miss out on any special offers or new releases.

•Links to follow me on Amazon or social media to be kept up to date with new releases.

•Free books and bonus content.

•Opportunities to read my books before they are even released by joining my team.

•Sneak peeks at new material before anyone else.

stellaandrews.com

Follow me on Amazon

Made in the USA
Middletown, DE
19 April 2024